Jeremy K.

FANG FAIRY

written and illustrated by Andy J. Smith

Librarian Reviewer

Katharine Kan
Graphic novel reviewer and Library Consultant, Panama City, FL
MLS in Library and Information Studies, University of Hawaii at
Manoa, HI

Reading Consultant

Elizabeth Stedem
Educator/Consultant, Colorado Springs, CO
MA in Elementary Education, University of Denver, CO

 STONE ARCH BOOKS
MINNEAPOLIS   SAN DIEGO

Graphic Sparks are published by Stone Arch Books,
A Capstone Imprint
1710 Roe Crest Drive
North Mankato, Minnesota 56003
www.capstonepub.com

Library of Congress Cataloging-in-Publication Data
Smith, Andy J., 1975–
   Fang Fairy / by Andy J. Smith; illustrated by Andy J. Smith.
   p. cm. — (Graphic Sparks. Jeremy Kreep)
   ISBN-13: 978-1-59889-835-4 (library binding)
   ISBN-10: 1-59889-835-3 (library binding)
   ISBN-13: 978-1-59889-891-0 (paperback)
   ISBN-10: 1-59889-891-4 (paperback)
   1. Graphic novels. I. Title.
PN6727.S5456F36 2008
741.5'973—dc22   2007003176

Summary: Jeremy Kreep has a problem. Something snagged a baby tooth from beneath his
brother's pillow and left a puddle of slime! Now Jeremy and his best friend Nessy go off
to find the truth behind the tooth fairy. Is the creature just a silly superstition or a real-life
collector of fangs?

Art Director: Heather Kindseth
Graphic Designer: Brann Garvey

Printed in the United States of America in North Mankato, Minnesota.
052012
006736R

Jeremy Kreep
FANG FAIRY

written and illustrated
by Andy J. Smith

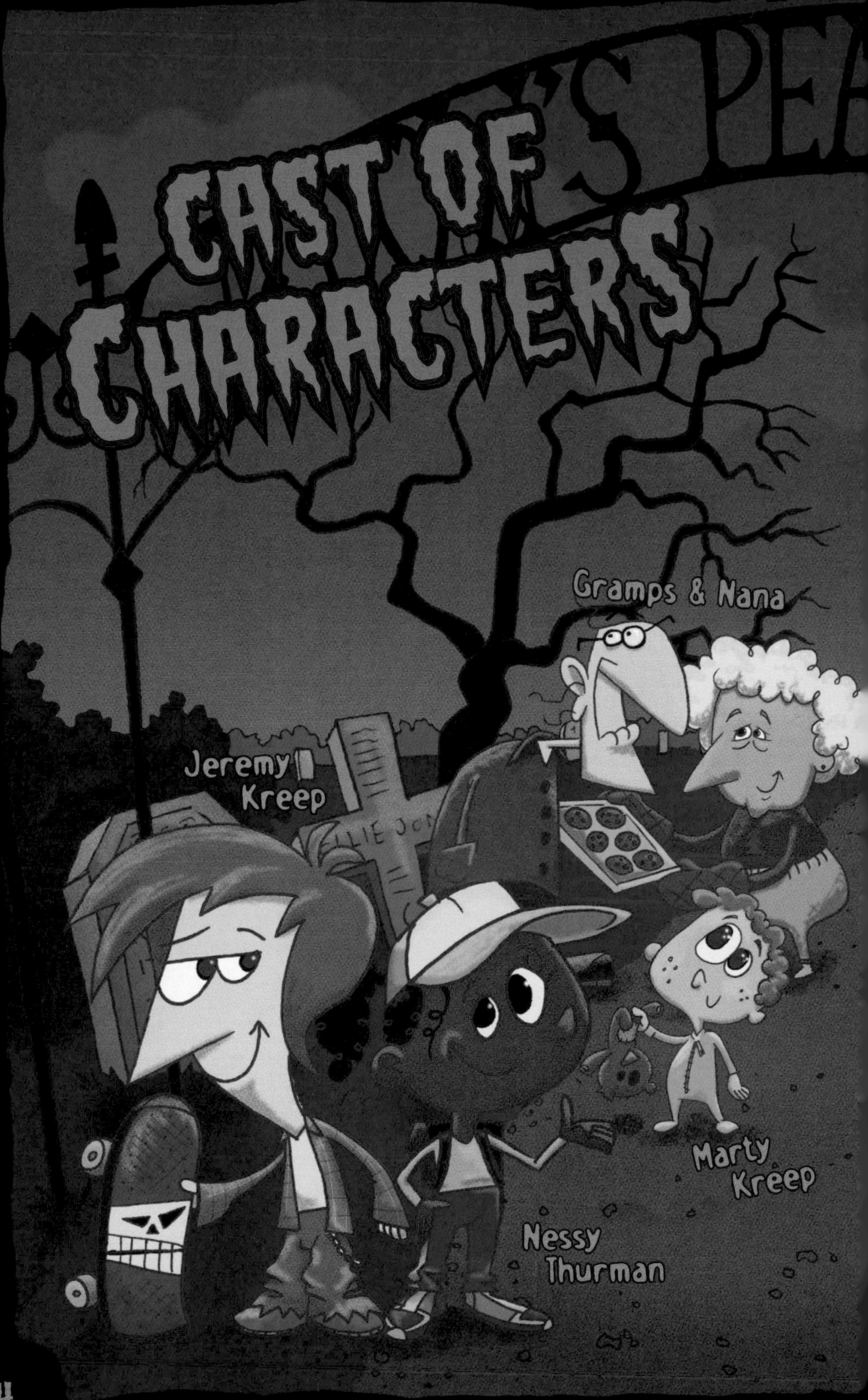
CAST OF CHARACTERS
Gramps & Nana
Jeremy Kreep
Marty Kreep
Nessy Thurman

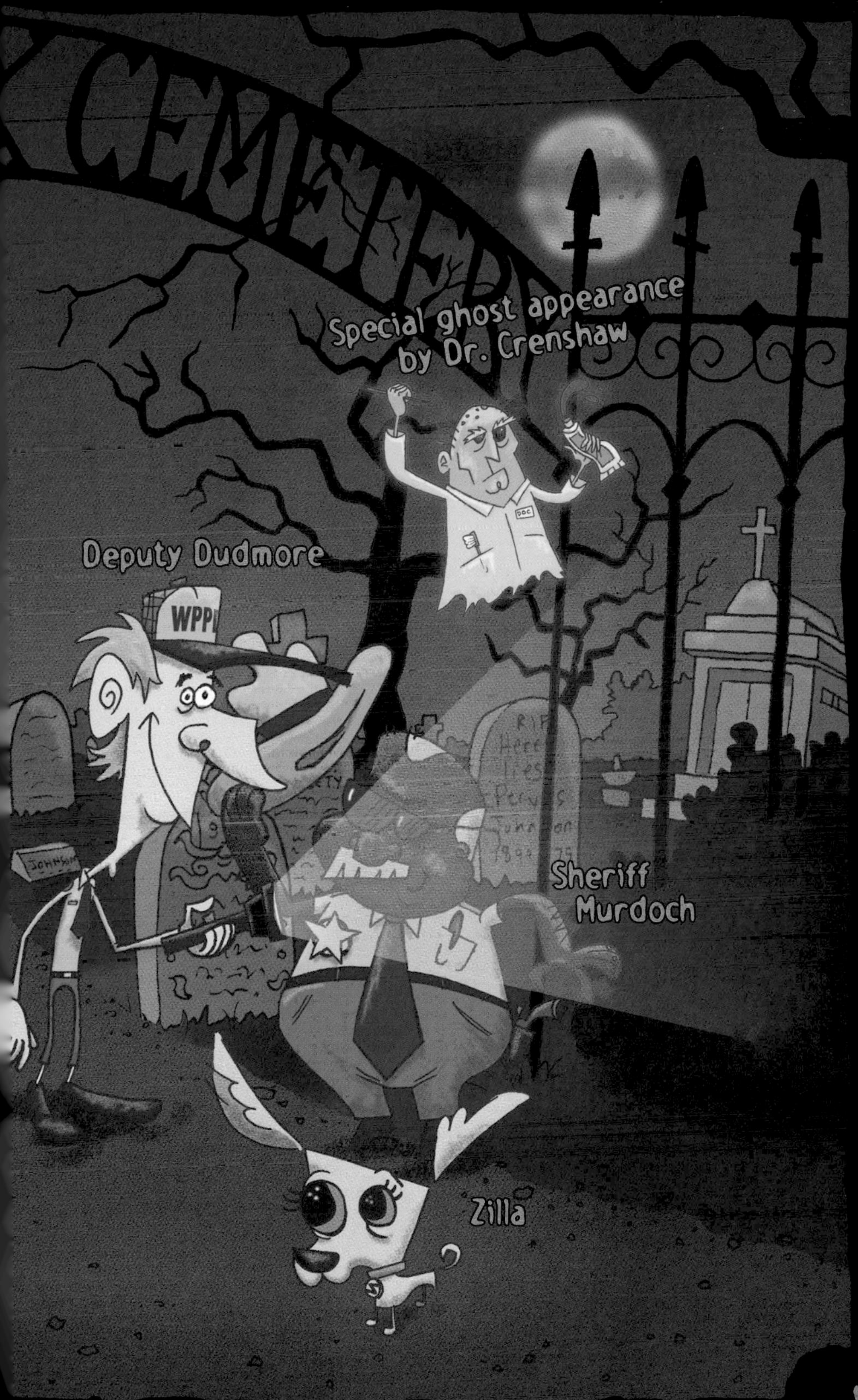
CEMETERY
Special ghost appearance by Dr. Crenshaw
Deputy Dudmore
WPPD
Sheriff Murdoch
Zilla

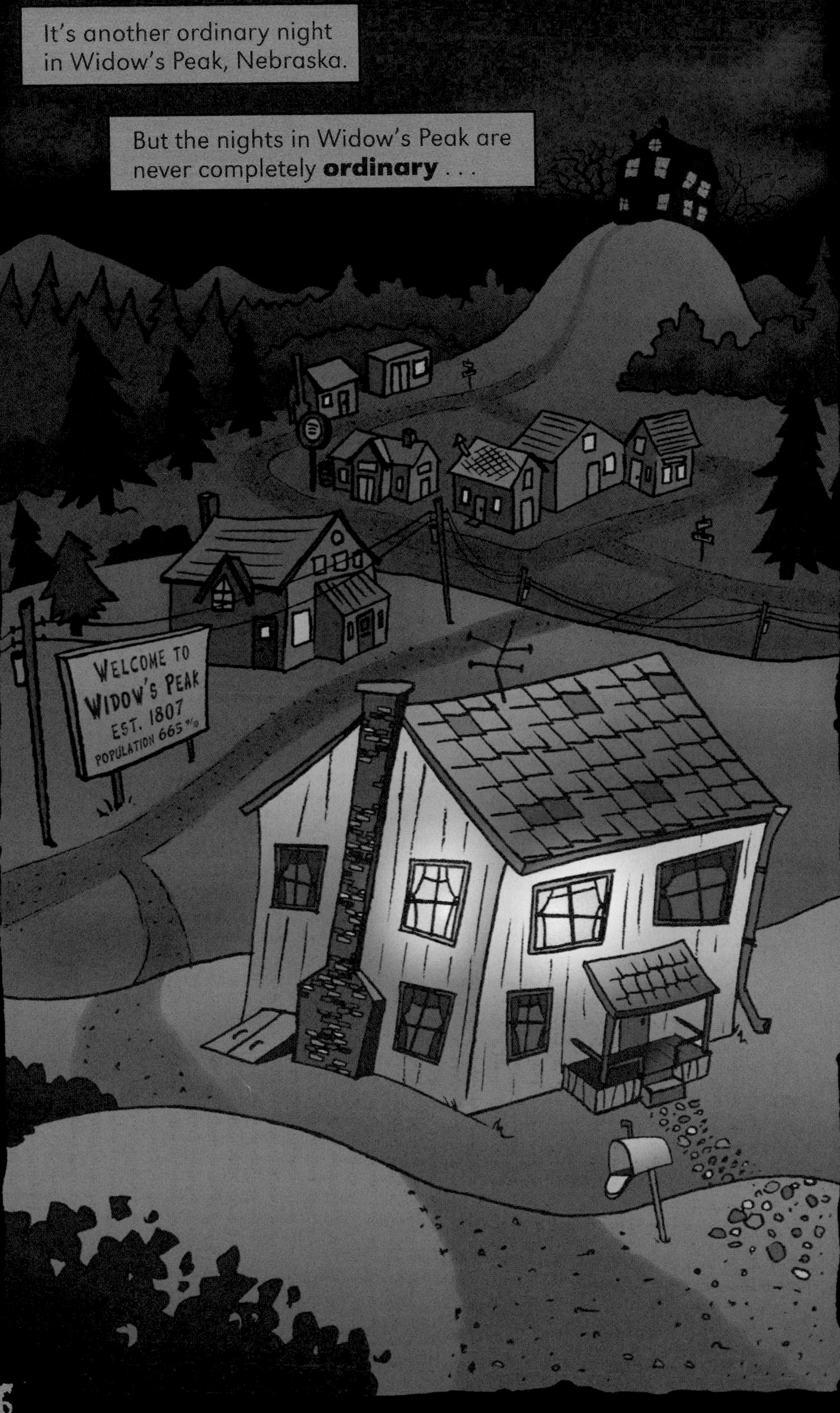
It's another ordinary night in Widow's Peak, Nebraska.
But the nights in Widow's Peak are never completely **ordinary** . . .
WELCOME TO WIDOW'S PEAK
EST. 1807
POPULATION 665

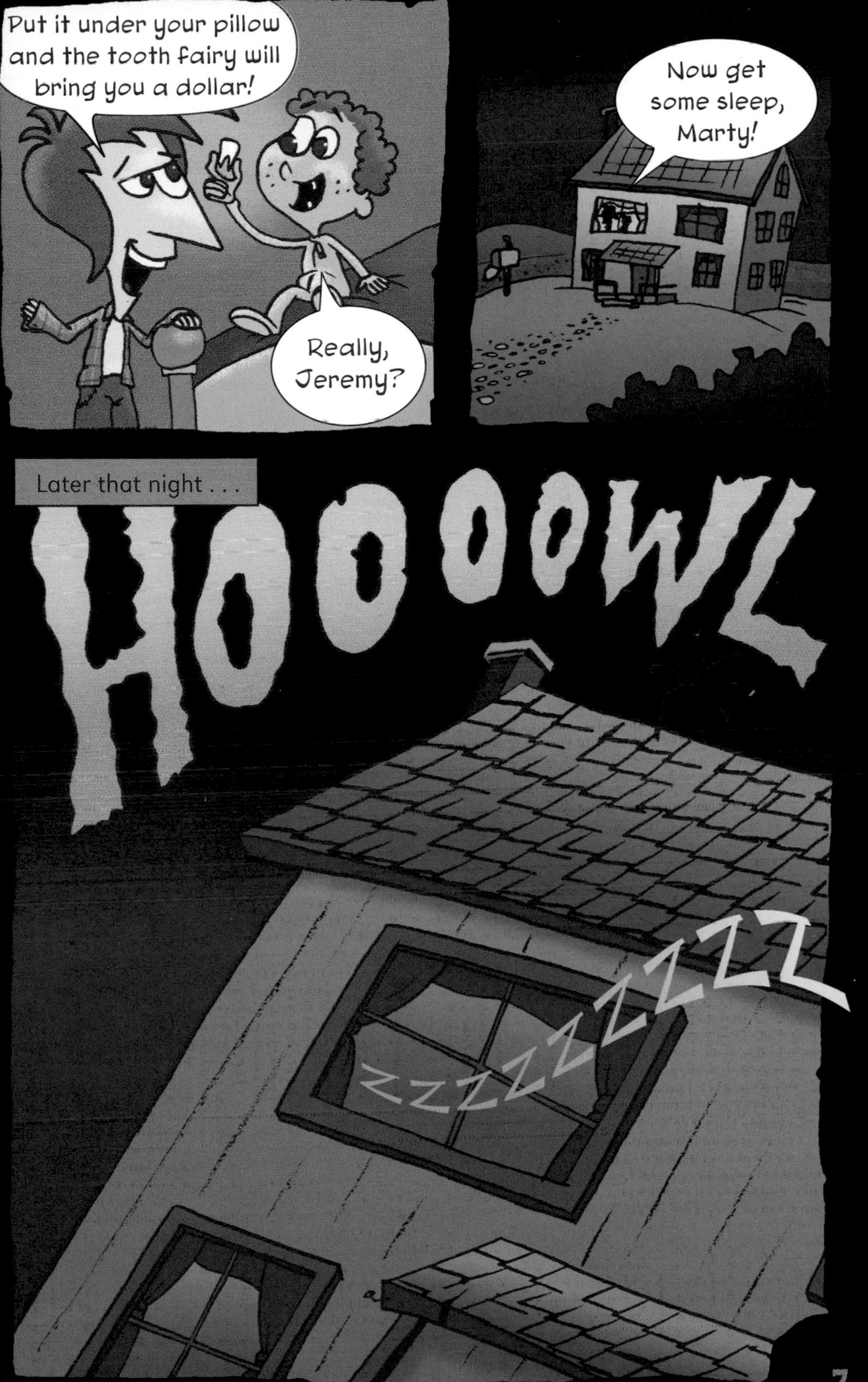
Put it under your pillow and the tooth fairy will bring you a dollar!
Really, Jeremy?
Now get some sleep, Marty!
Later that night . . .
HOOOOWL
ZZZZZZZZZZZ

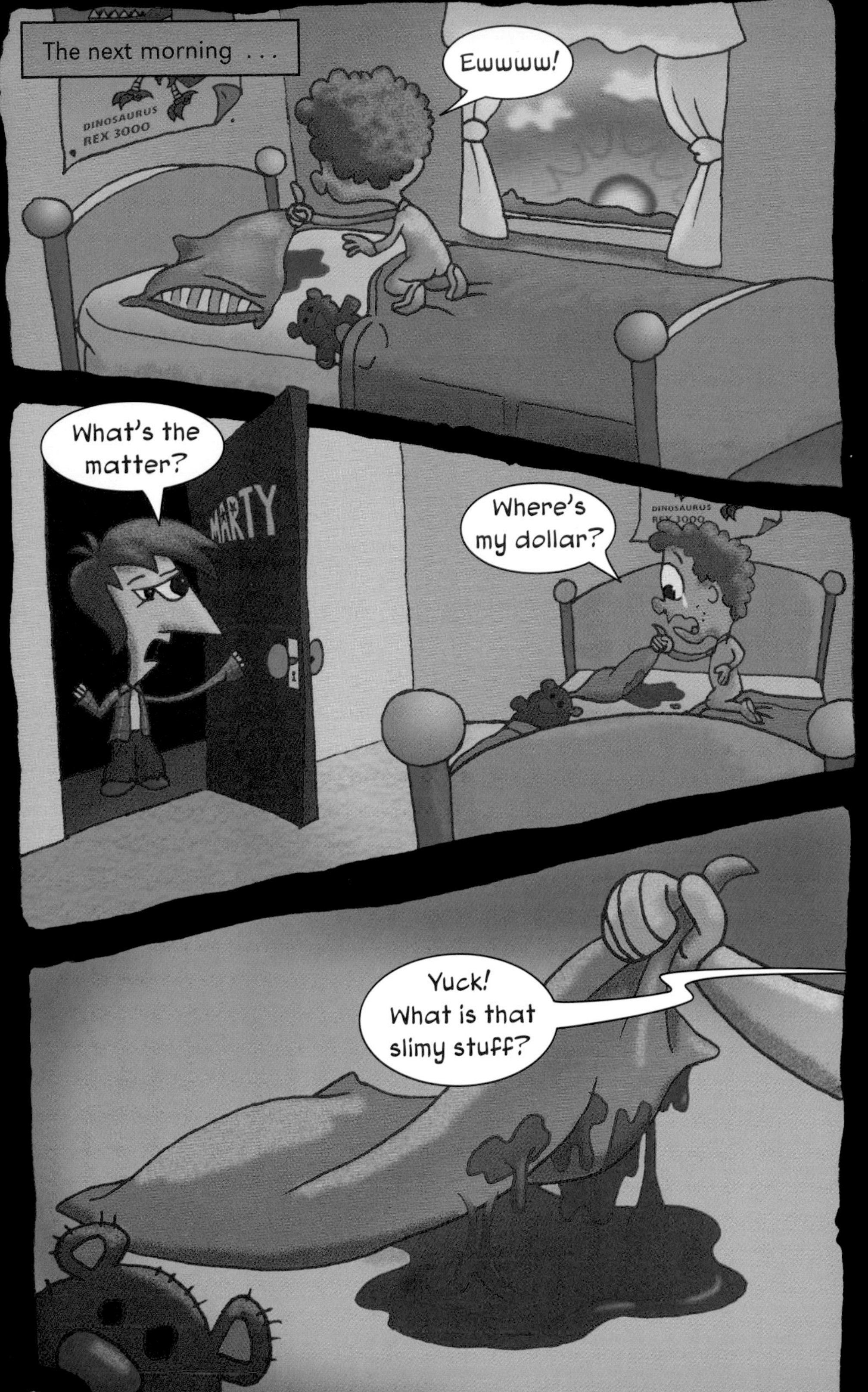
The next morning . . .
DINOSAURUS
REX 3000
Ewwww!
What's the matter?
MARTY
Where's my dollar?
Yuck! What is that slimy stuff?

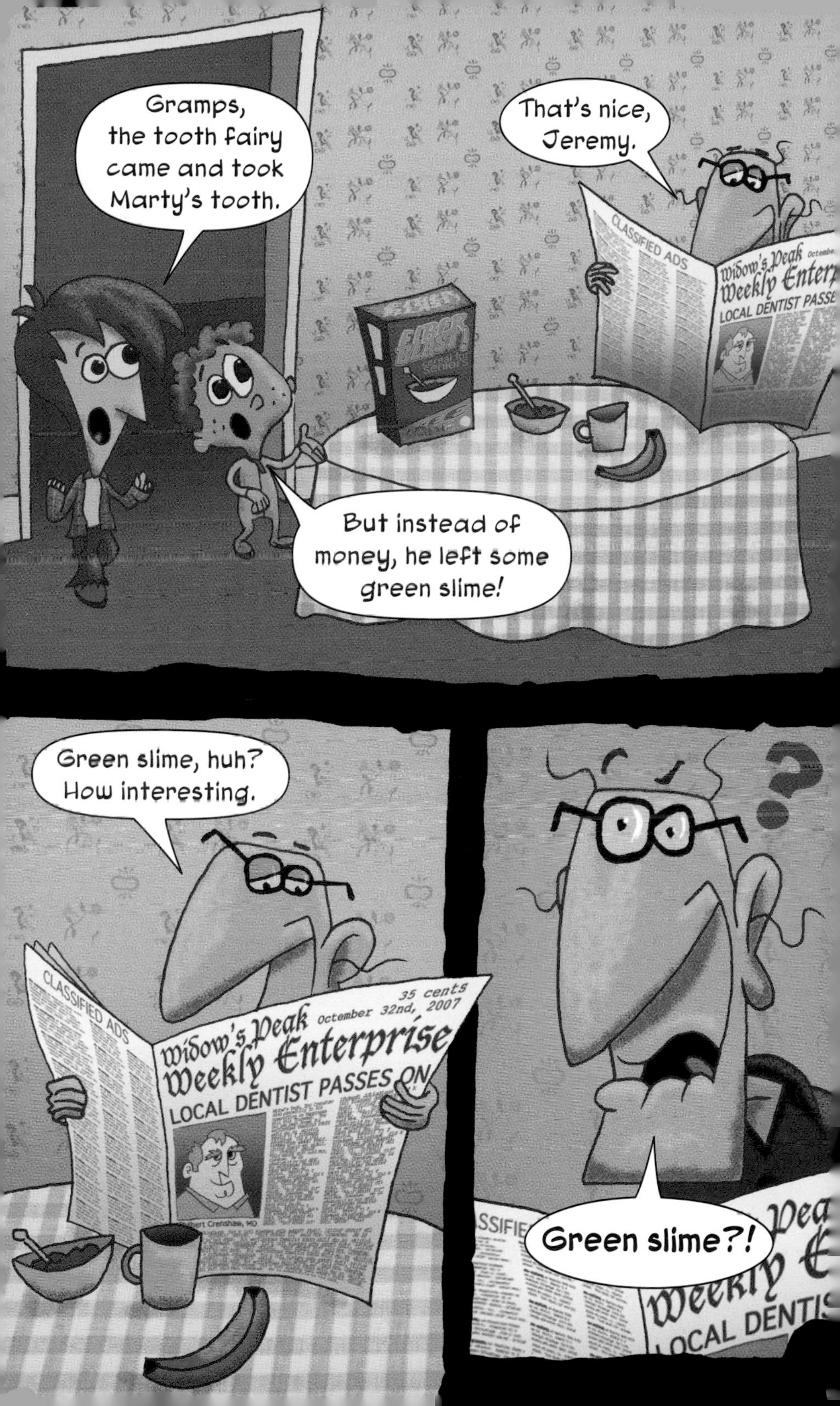
Gramps, the tooth fairy came and took Marty's tooth.
That's nice, Jeremy.
FIBER BLAST! cereal for seniors
CLASSIFIED ADS
But instead of money, he left some green slime!
Green slime, huh? How interesting.
CLASSIFIED ADS
35 cents
October 32nd, 2007
Widow's Peak Weekly Enterprise
LOCAL DENTIST PASSES ON
Green slime?!

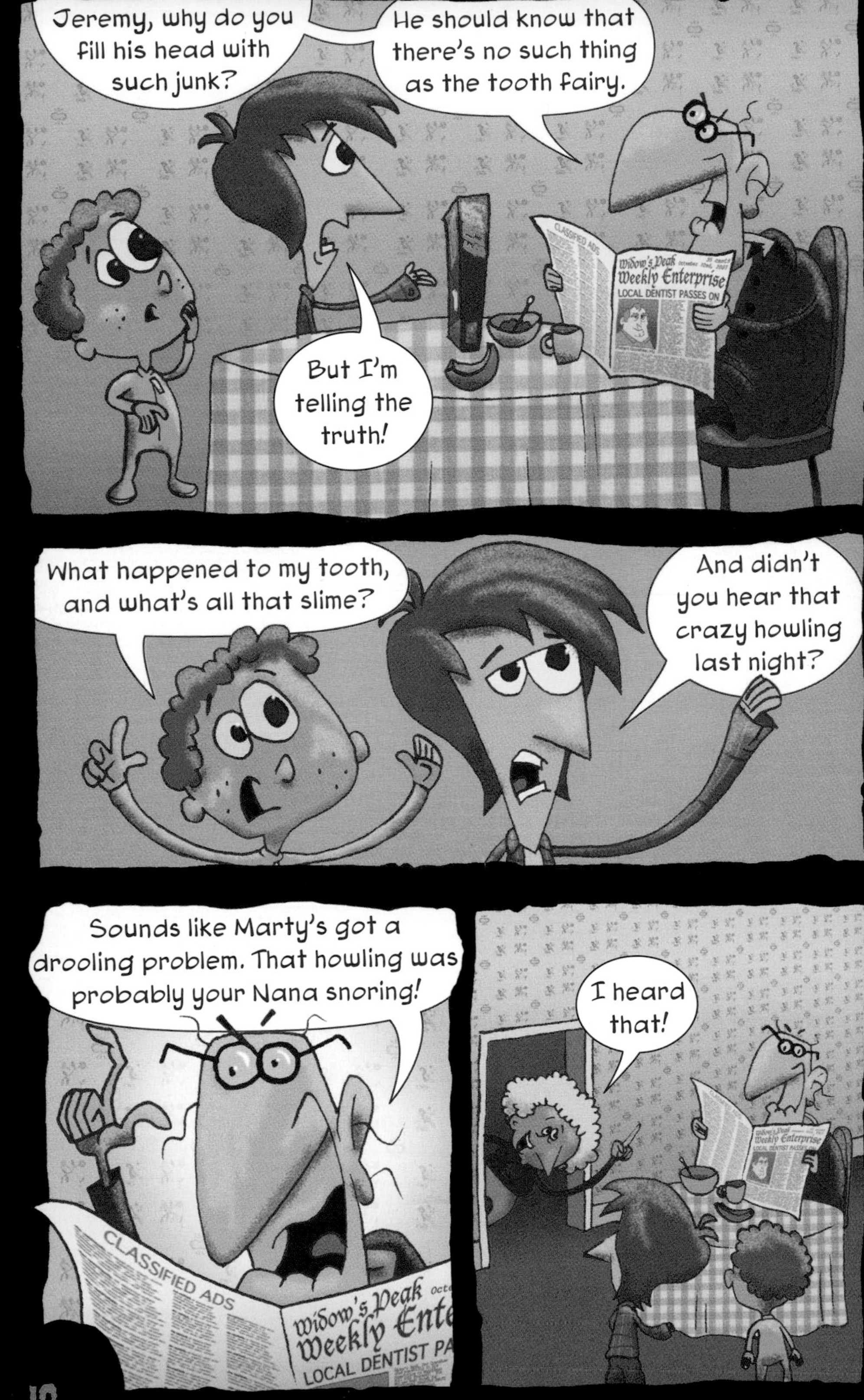

Jeremy, why do you fill his head with such junk?
He should know that there's no such thing as the tooth fairy.
But I'm telling the truth!
CLASSIFIED ADS
Widow's Peak Weekly Enterprise
LOCAL DENTIST PASSES ON
What happened to my tooth, and what's all that slime?
And didn't you hear that crazy howling last night?
Sounds like Marty's got a drooling problem. That howling was probably your Nana snoring!
CLASSIFIED ADS
Widow's Peak
Weekly Ente
LOCAL DENTIST PA
I heard that!

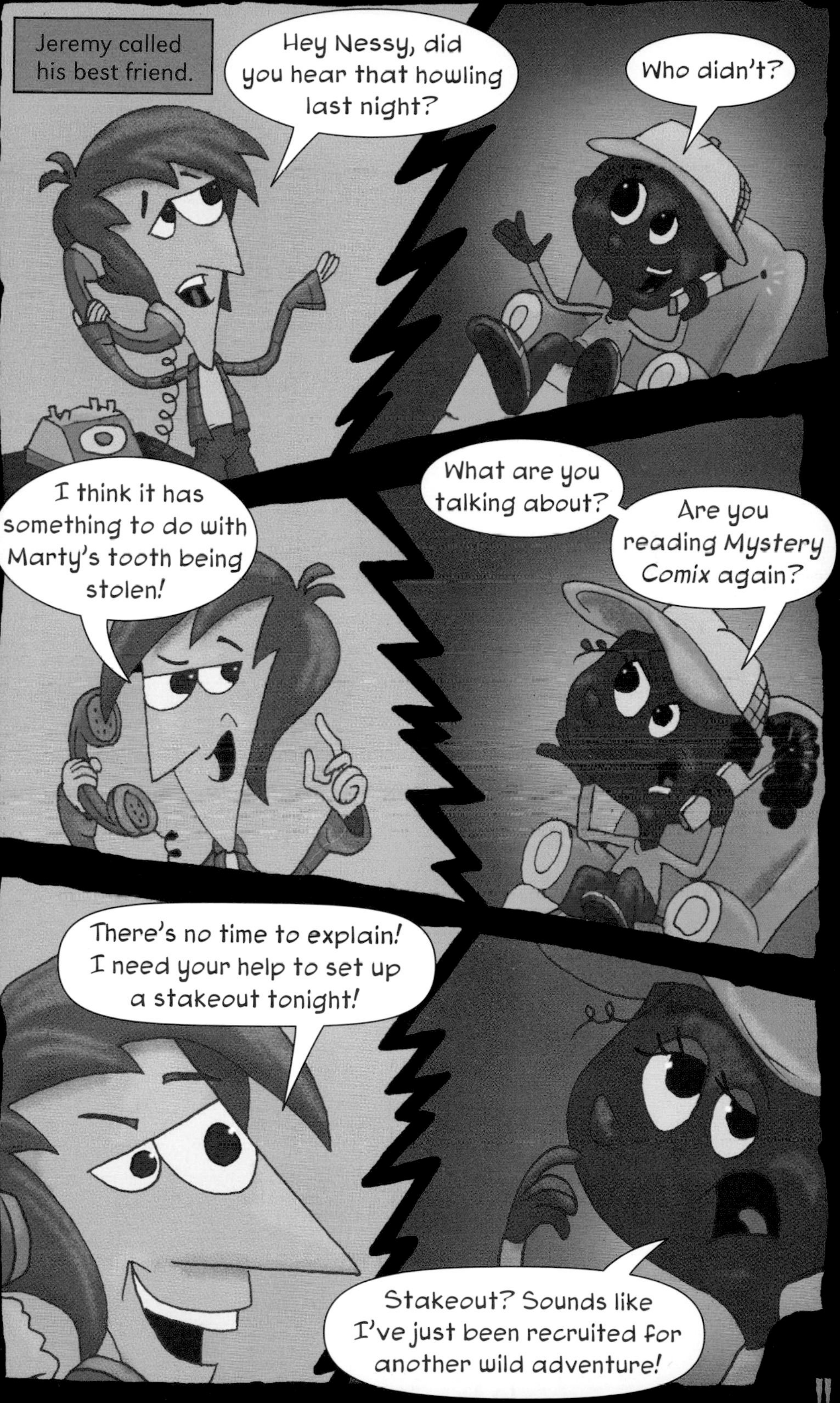

Jeremy called his best friend.
Hey Nessy, did you hear that howling last night?
Who didn't?
I think it has something to do with Marty's tooth being stolen!
What are you talking about?
Are you reading Mystery Comix again?
There's no time to explain! I need your help to set up a stakeout tonight!
Stakeout? Sounds like I've just been recruited for another wild adventure!

That evening . . .

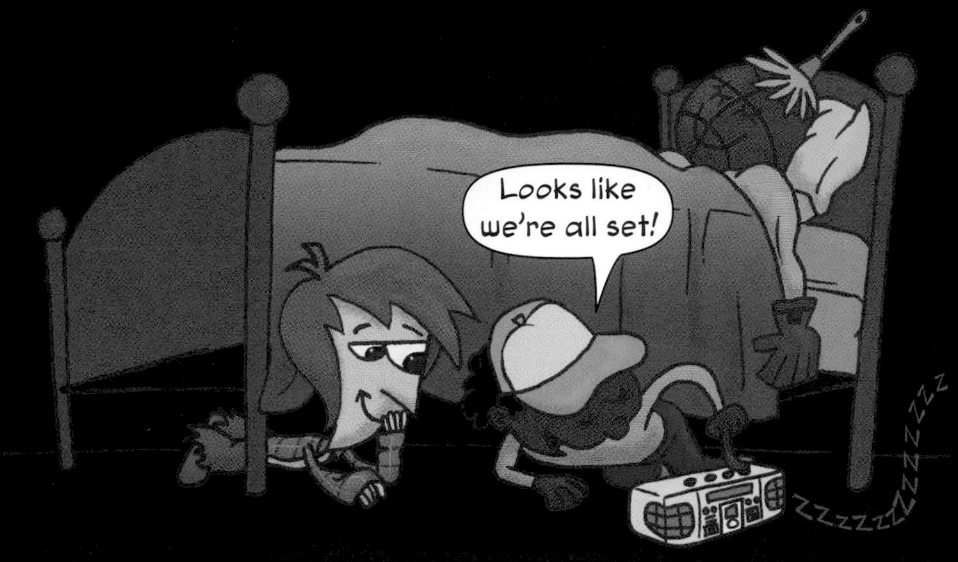
Looks like we're all set!
ZZzzzzzzzzzz

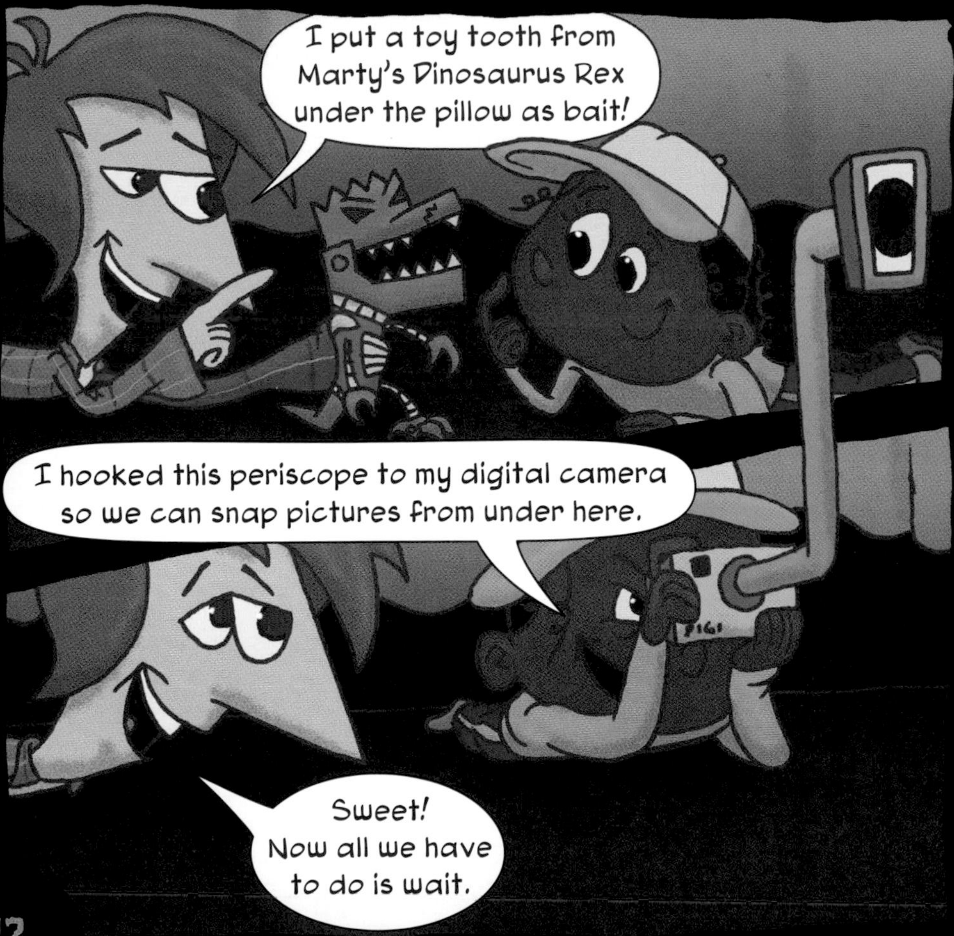
I put a toy tooth from Marty's Dinosaurus Rex under the pillow as bait!
I hooked this periscope to my digital camera so we can snap pictures from under here.
Sweet! Now all we have to do is wait.

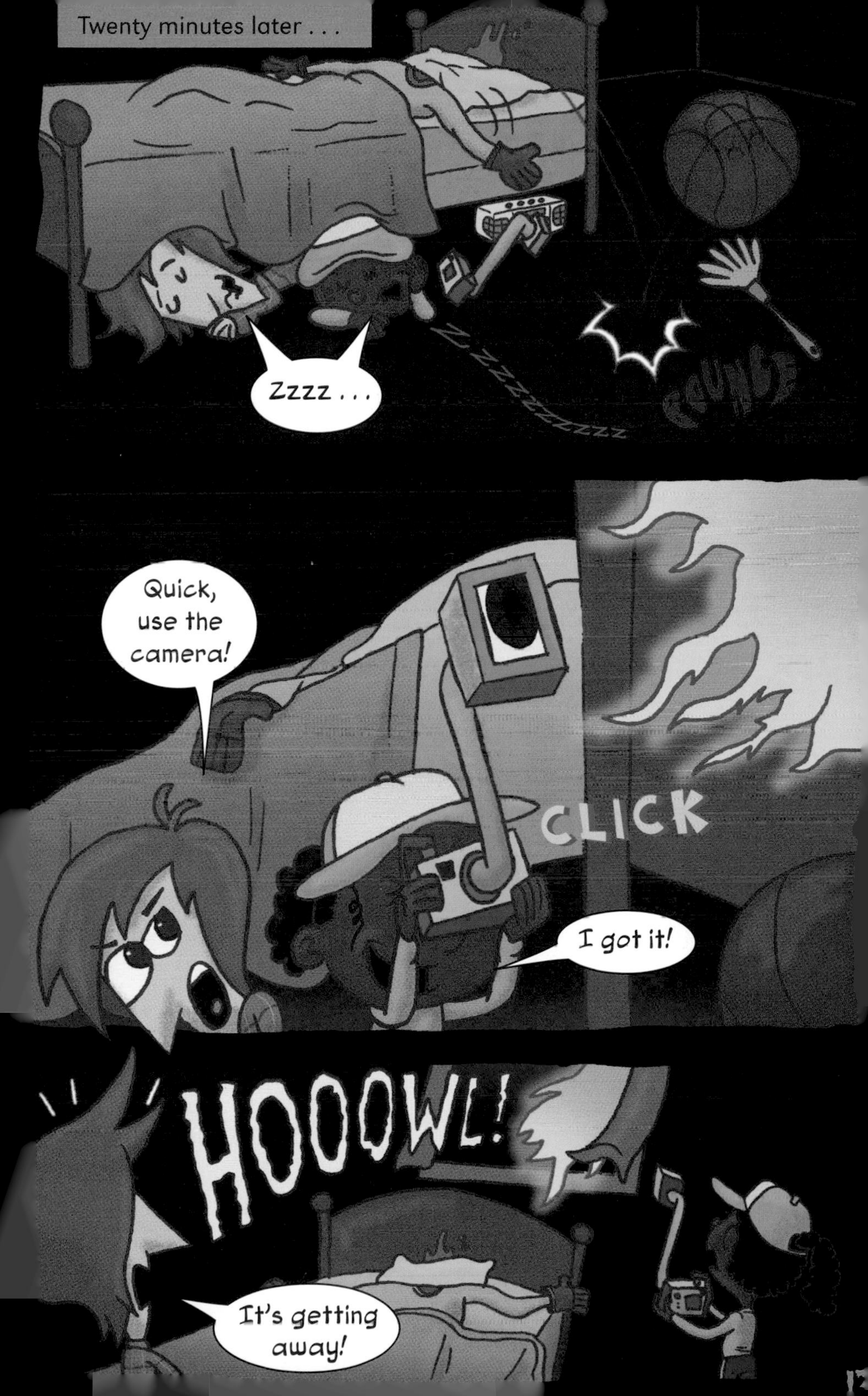
Twenty minutes later . . .
Zzzz . . .
Quick, use the camera!
CLICK
I got it!
HOOOWL!
It's getting away!

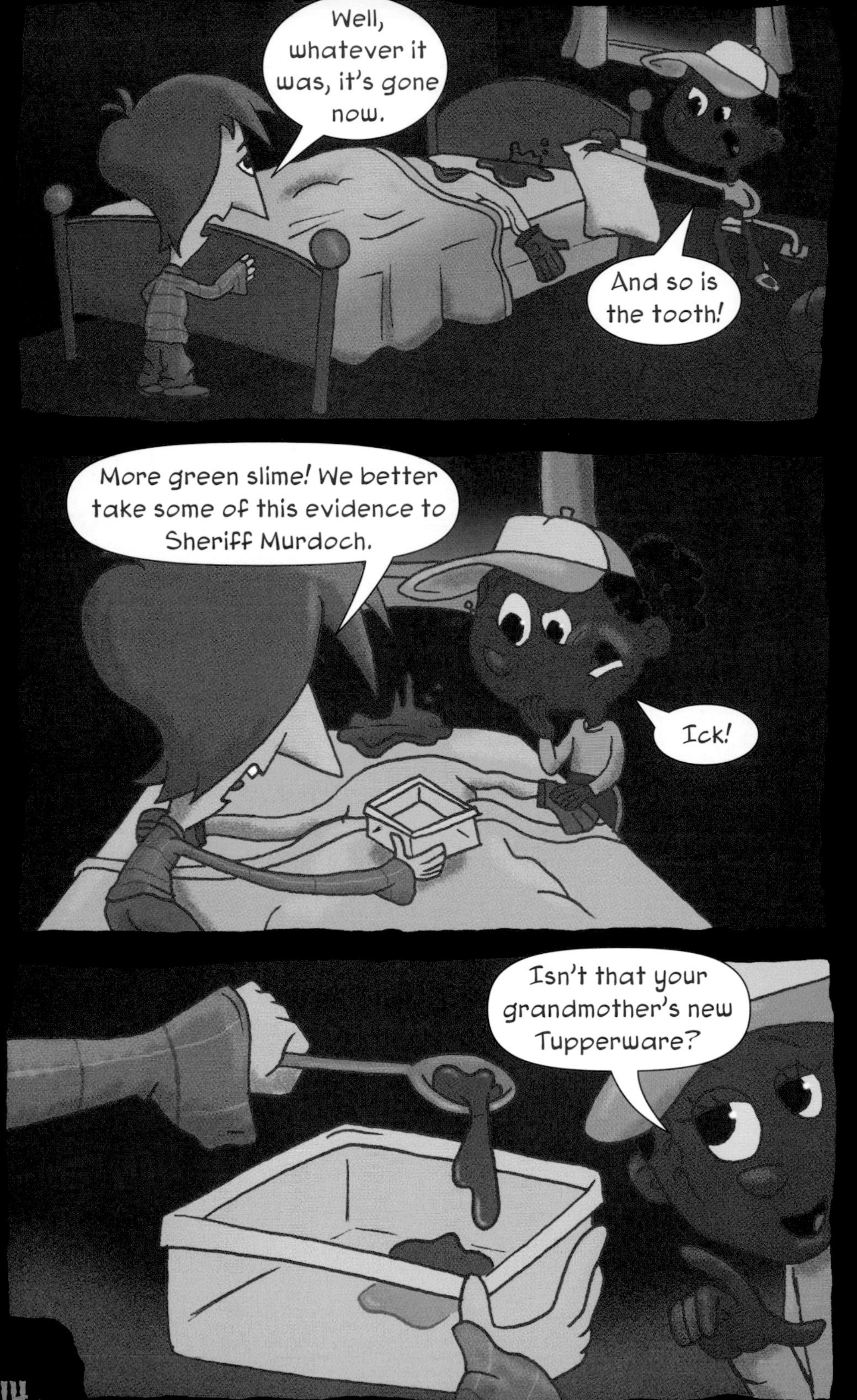
Well, whatever it was, it's gone now.
And so is the tooth!
More green slime! We better take some of this evidence to Sheriff Murdoch.
Ick!
Isn't that your grandmother's new Tupperware?

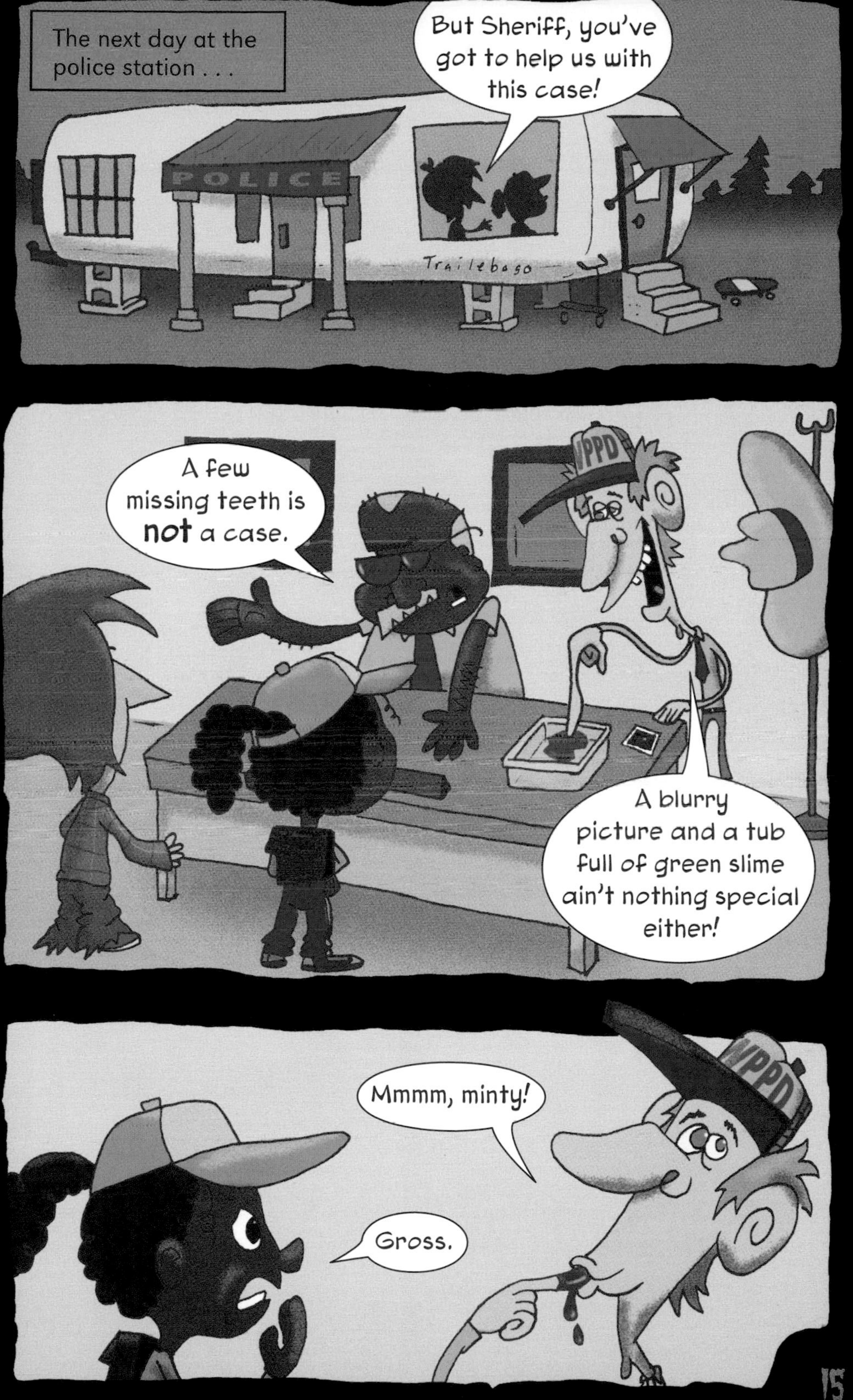

The next day at the police station . . .
POLICE
But Sheriff, you've got to help us with this case!
A few missing teeth is **not** a case.
A blurry picture and a tub full of green slime ain't nothing special either!
Mmmm, minty!
Gross.

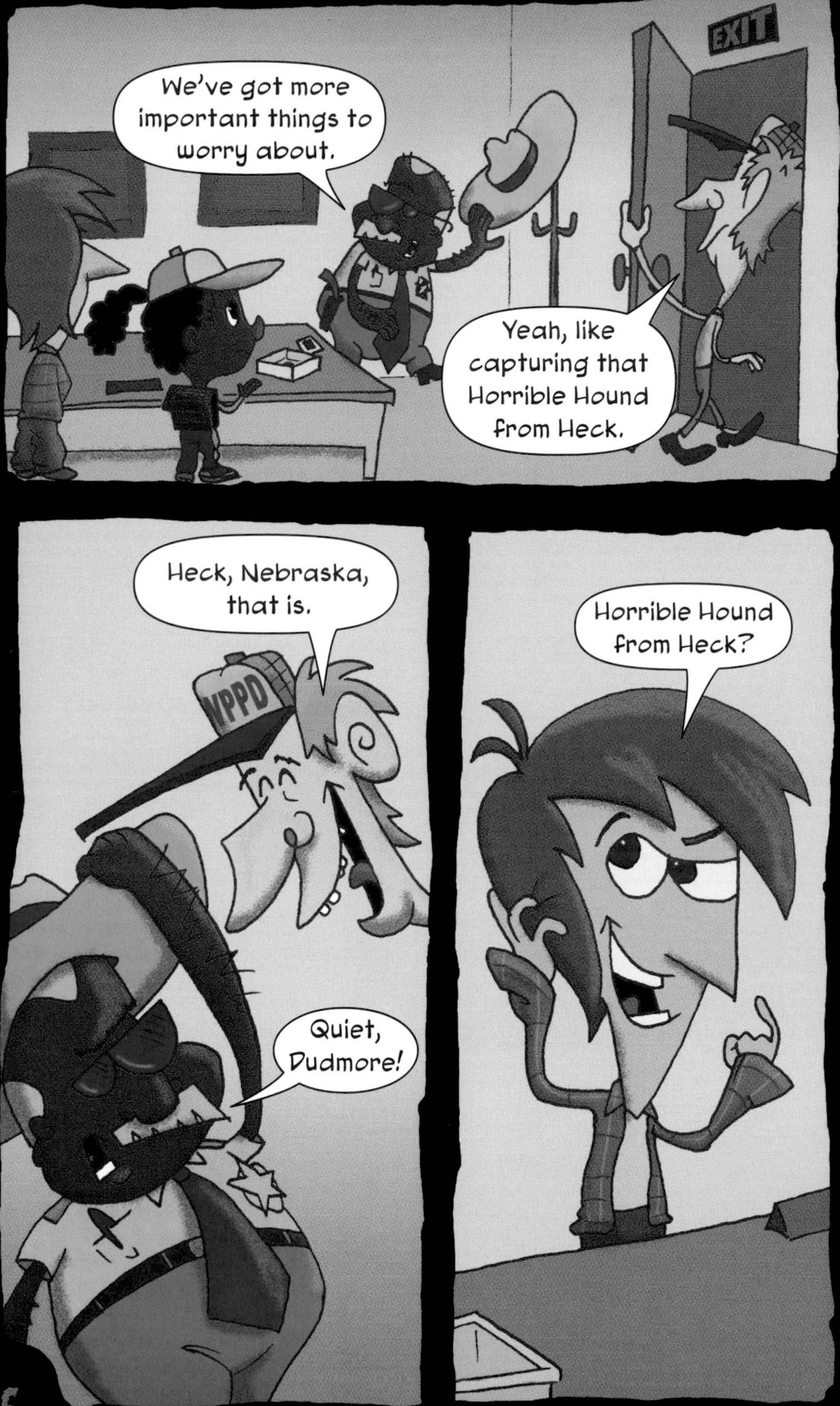
We've got more important things to worry about.
Yeah, like capturing that Horrible Hound from Heck.
Heck, Nebraska, that is.
Quiet, Dudmore!
Horrible Hound from Heck?

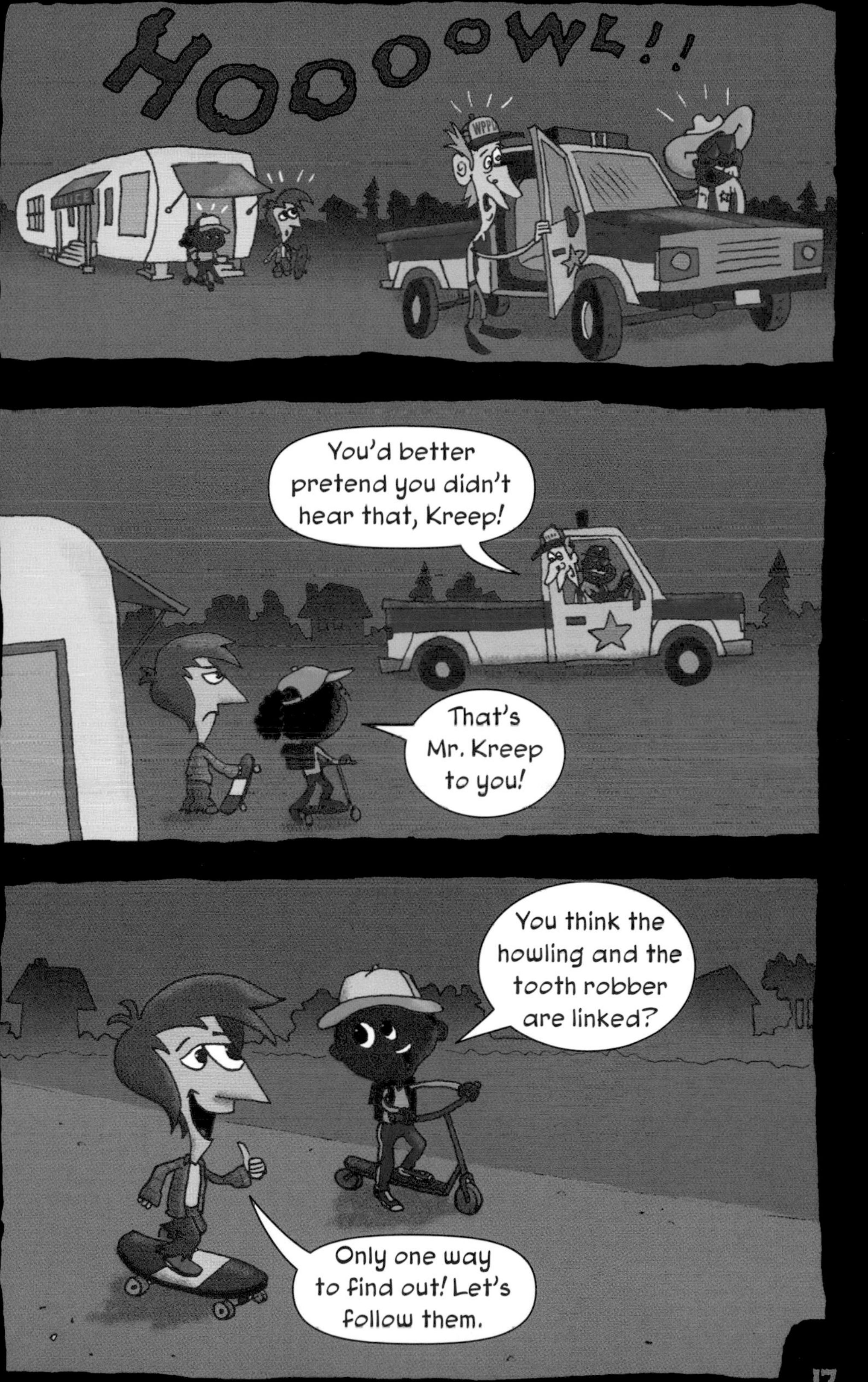
HOOOOOWL!!
WPPD
POLICE
You'd better pretend you didn't hear that, Kreep!
That's Mr. Kreep to you!
You think the howling and the tooth robber are linked?
Only one way to find out! Let's follow them.

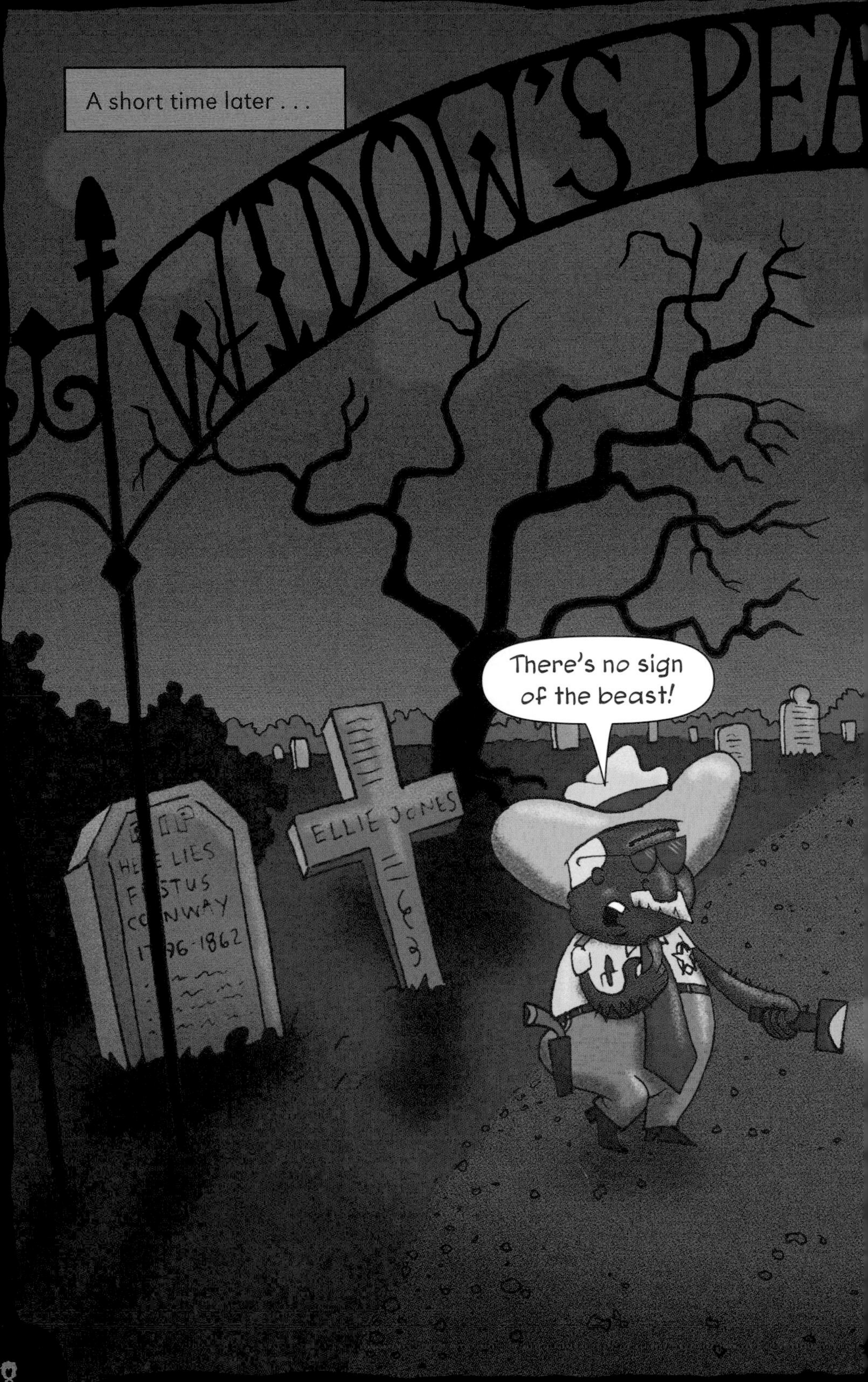
A short time later . . .
WIDOW'S PEA
ELLIE JONES
There's no sign of the beast!

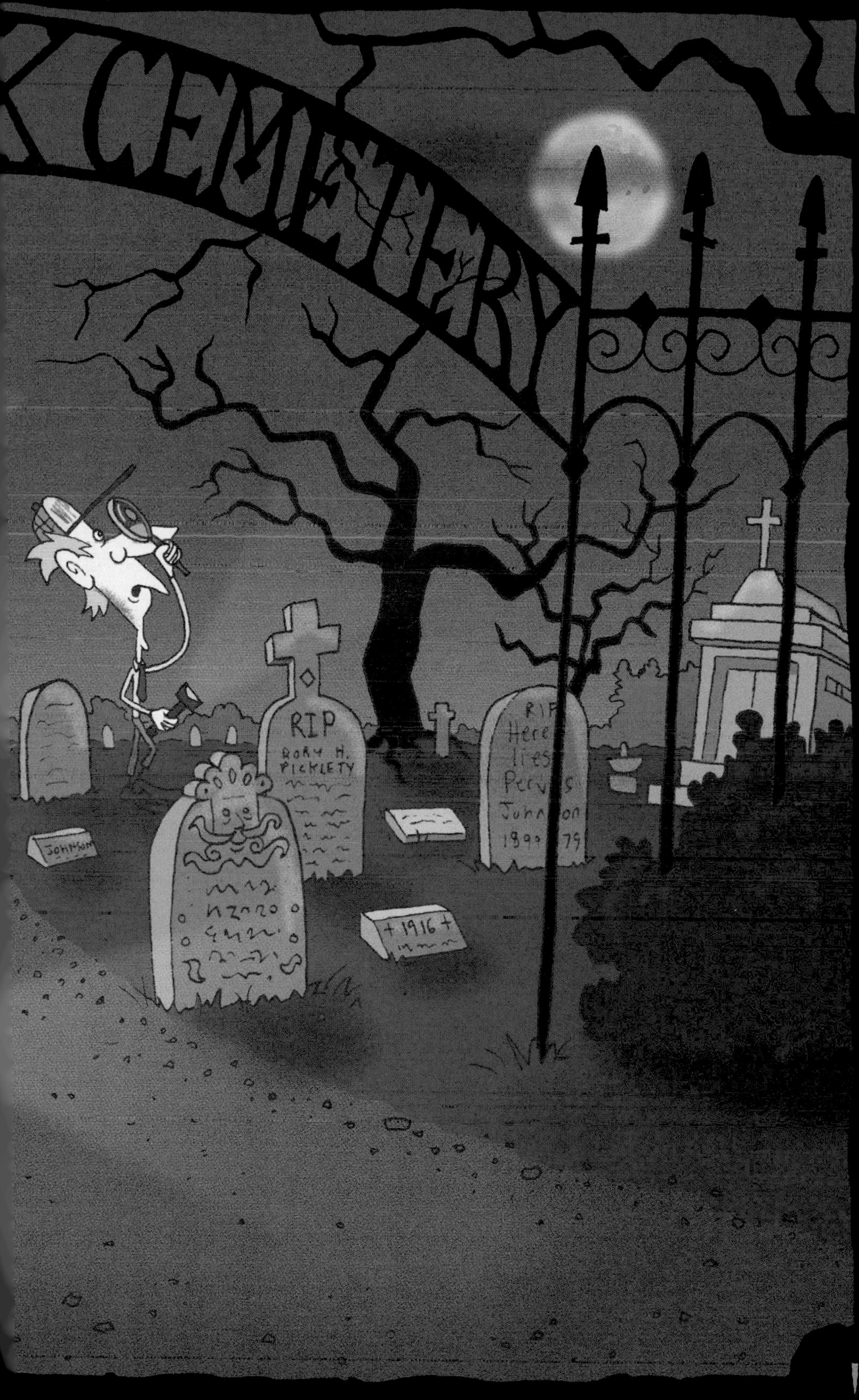
CEMETERY
RIP
RORY H. PICKLETY
JOHNSON
+1916+

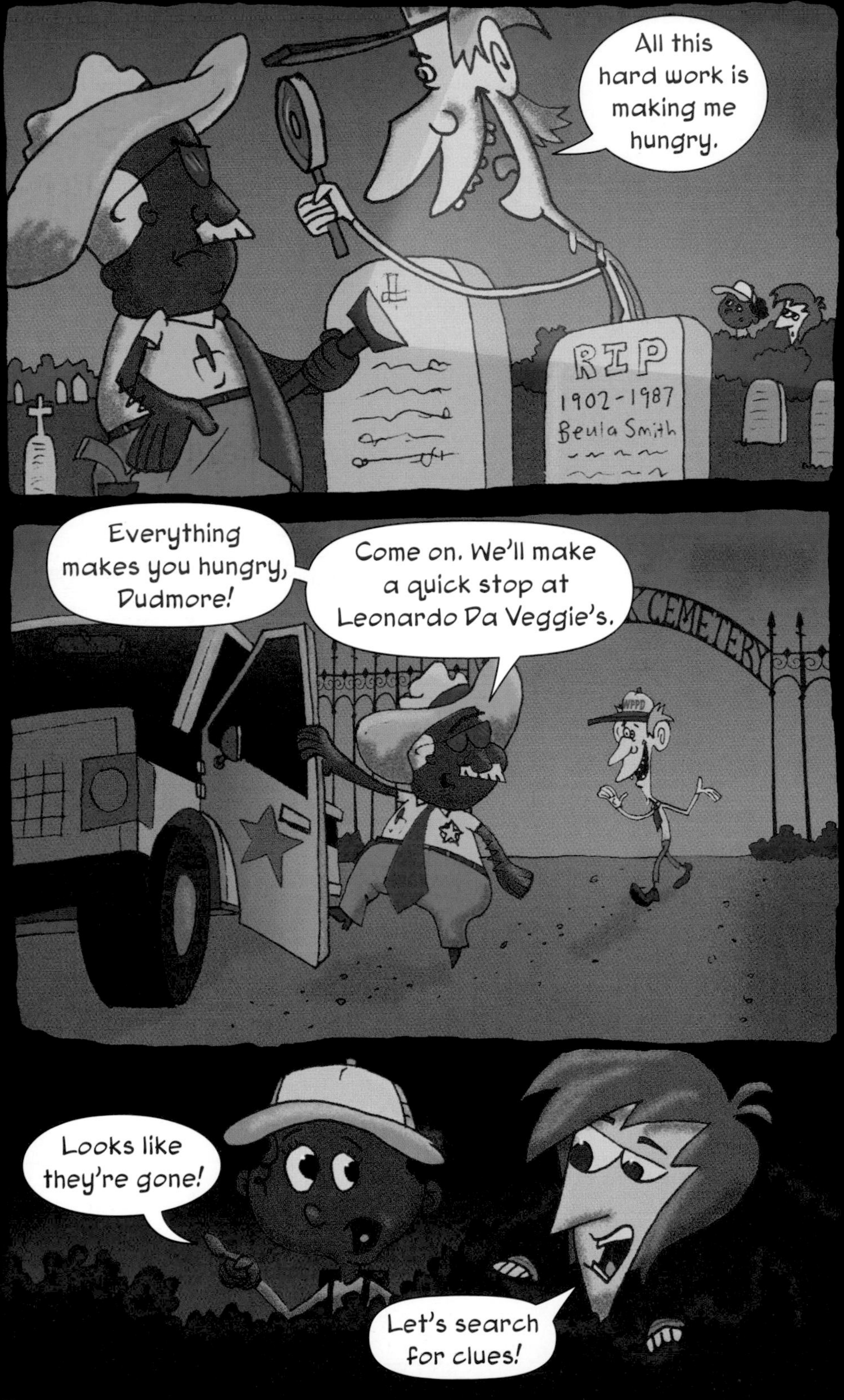
All this hard work is making me hungry.
RIP
1902-1987
Beula Smith
Everything makes you hungry, Dudmore!
Come on. We'll make a quick stop at Leonardo Da Veggie's.
CEMETERY
WPPD
Looks like they're gone!
Let's search for clues!

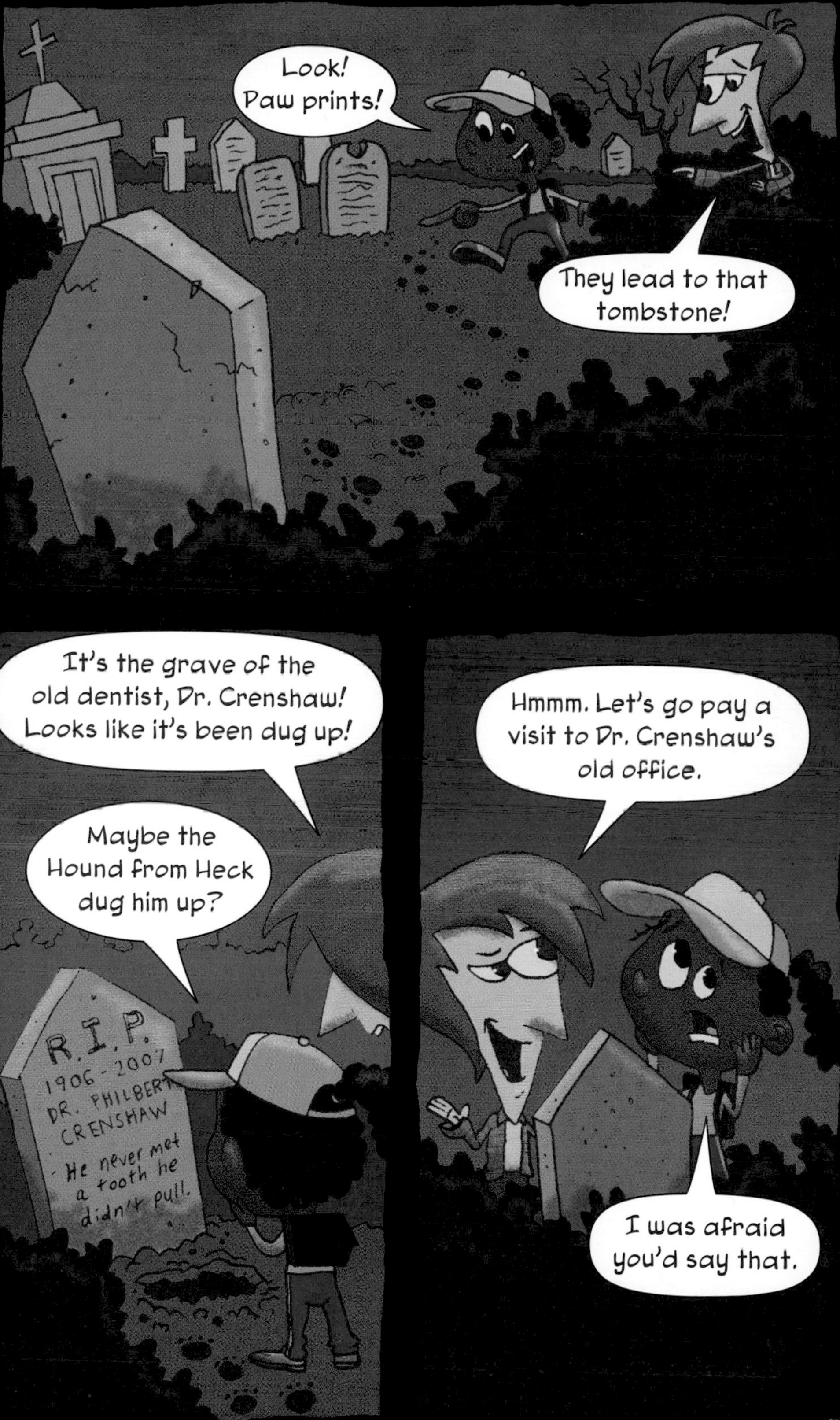
Look! Paw prints!
They lead to that tombstone!
It's the grave of the old dentist, Dr. Crenshaw! Looks like it's been dug up!
Maybe the Hound from Heck dug him up?
R.I.P.
1906 - 2007
DR. PHILBERT CRENSHAW
He never met a tooth he didn't pull.
Hmmm. Let's go pay a visit to Dr. Crenshaw's old office.
I was afraid you'd say that.

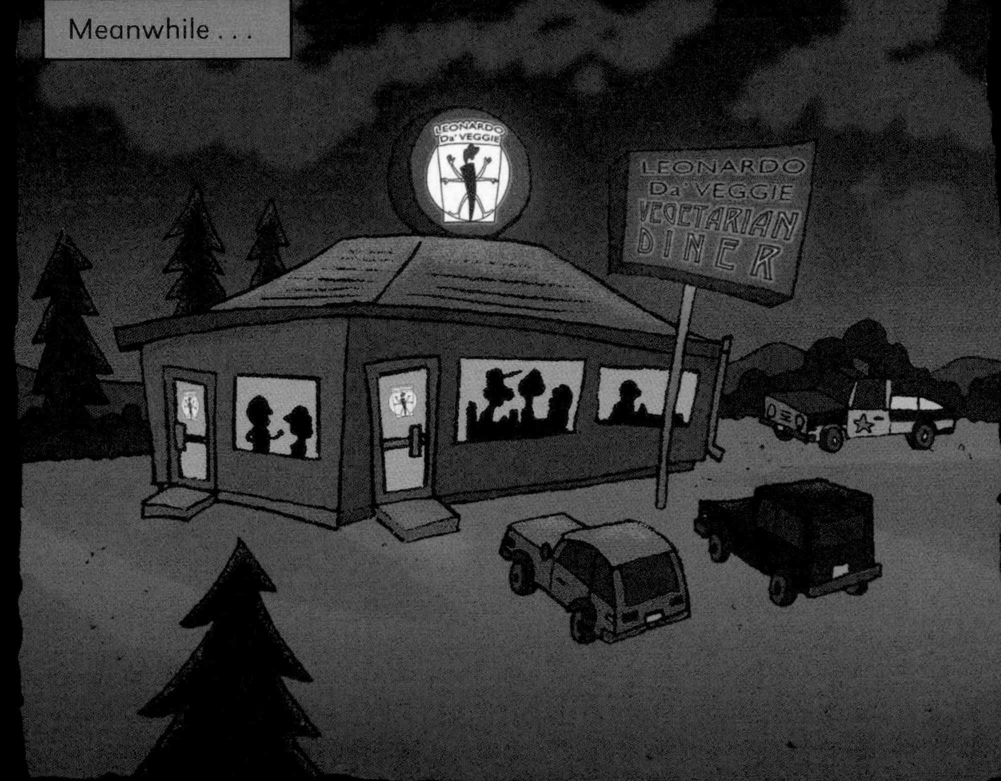
Meanwhile . . .
LEONARDO Da' VEGGIE
LEONARDO Da' VEGGIE VEGETARIAN DINER

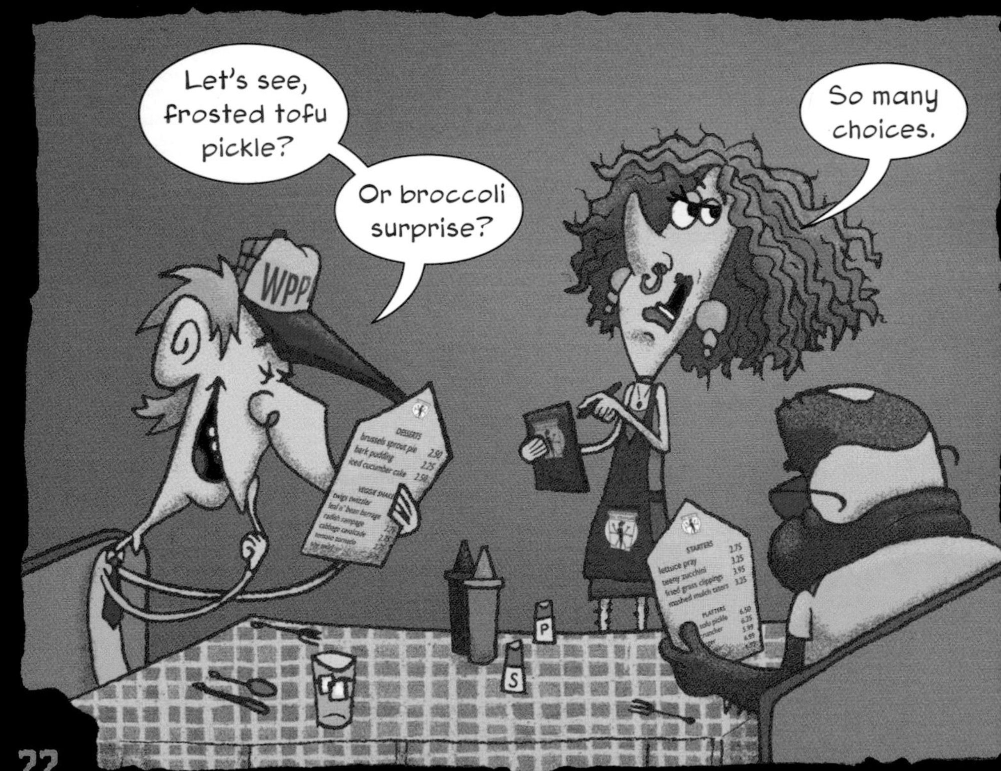
Let's see, frosted tofu pickle?
Or broccoli surprise?
So many choices.
WPP
DESSERTS
brussels sprout pie 2.50
bark pudding 2.25
iced cucumber cake 2.50
twigs twizzler
leaf n' bean barrage
radish rampage
cabbage cavalcade
tomato tornado
STARTERS
lettuce pray 2.75
teeny zucchini 3.25
fried grass clippings 3.95
mashed mulch taters 3.25
PLATTERS 6.50
tofu pickle 6.25
P
S

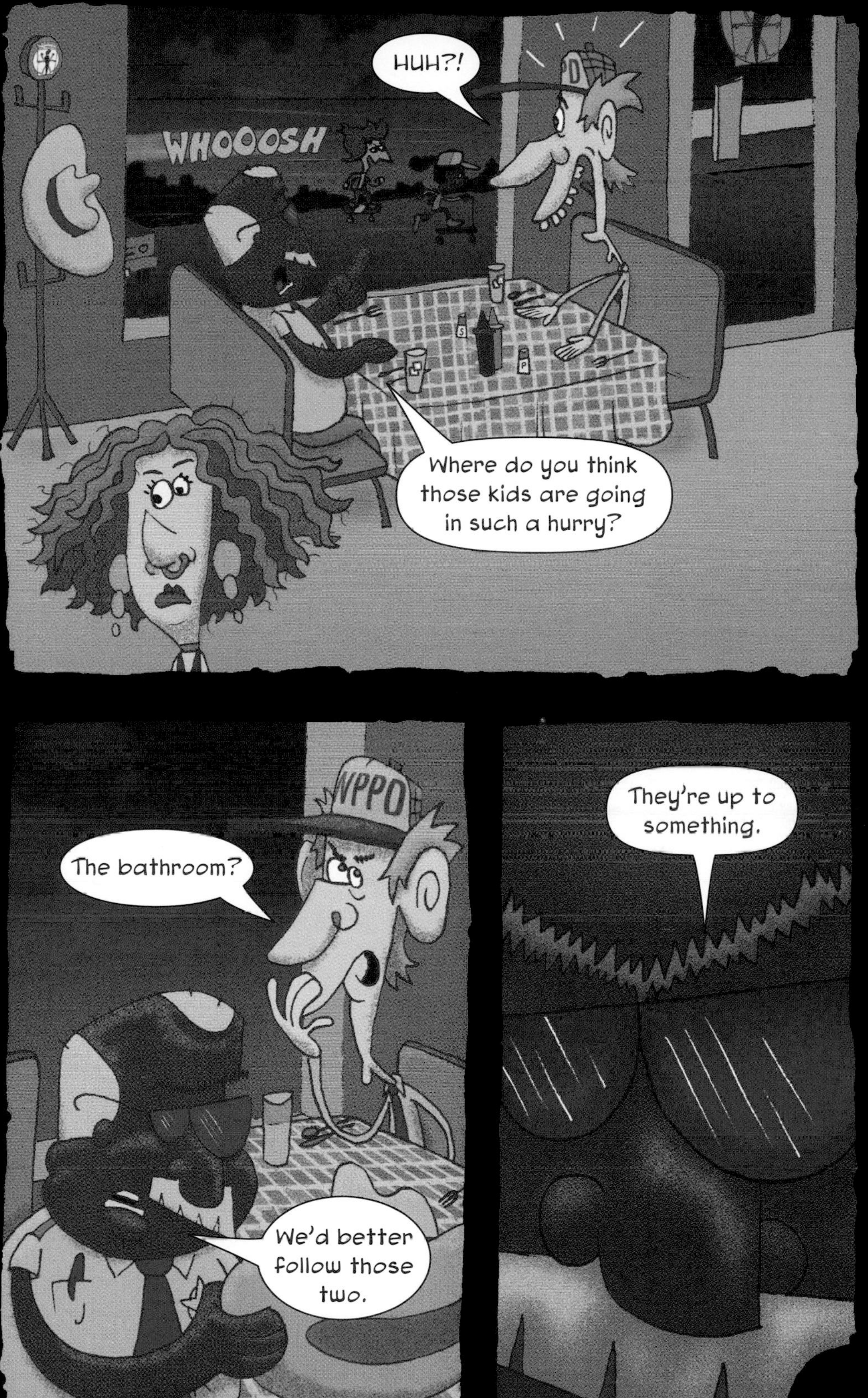
HUH?!
WHOOOSH
PD
Where do you think those kids are going in such a hurry?
WPPO
The bathroom?
We'd better follow those two.
They're up to something.

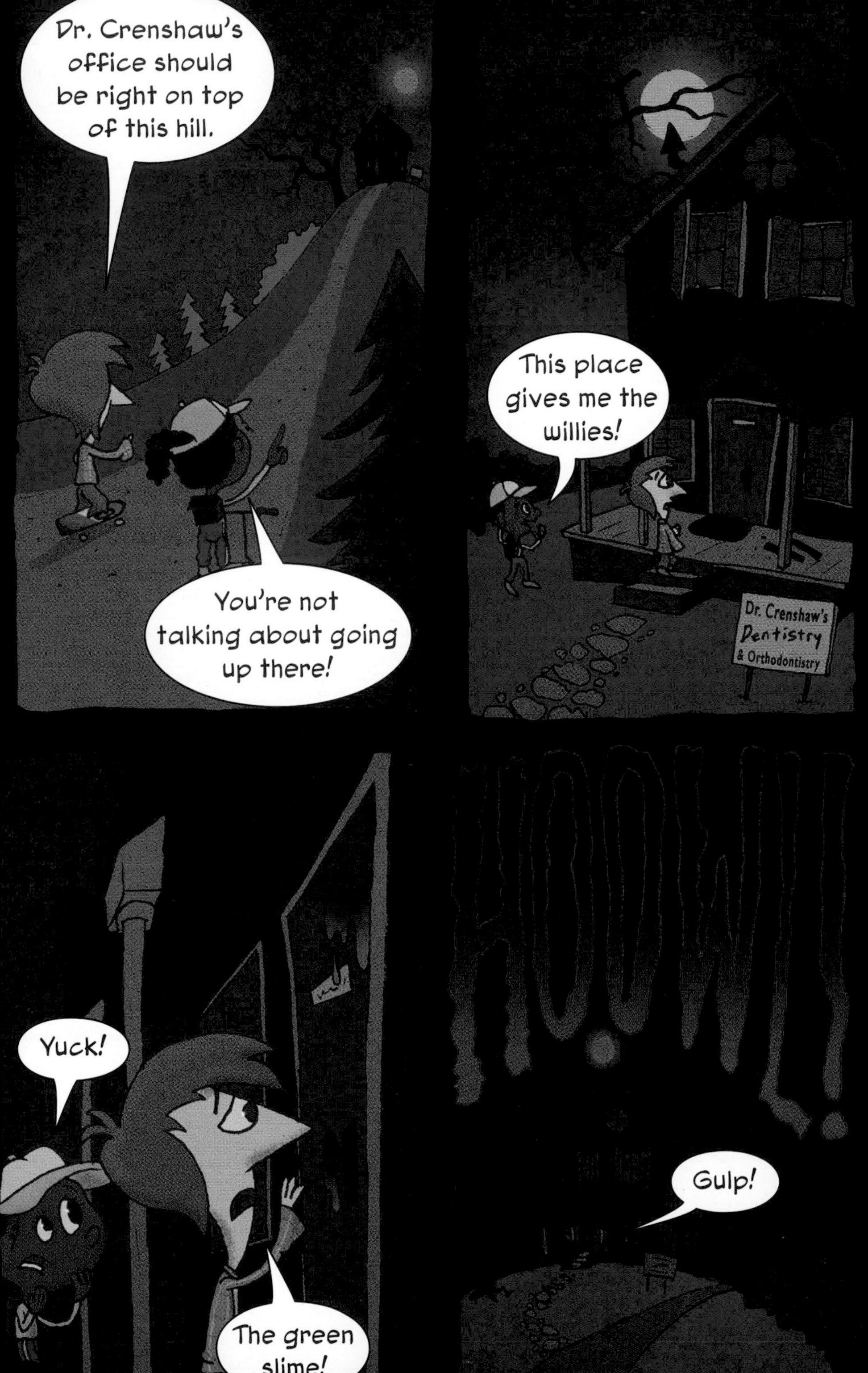
Dr. Crenshaw's office should be right on top of this hill.
You're not talking about going up there!
This place gives me the willies!
Dr. Crenshaw's Dentistry & Orthodontistry
Yuck!
The green slime!
HOOWL!
Gulp!

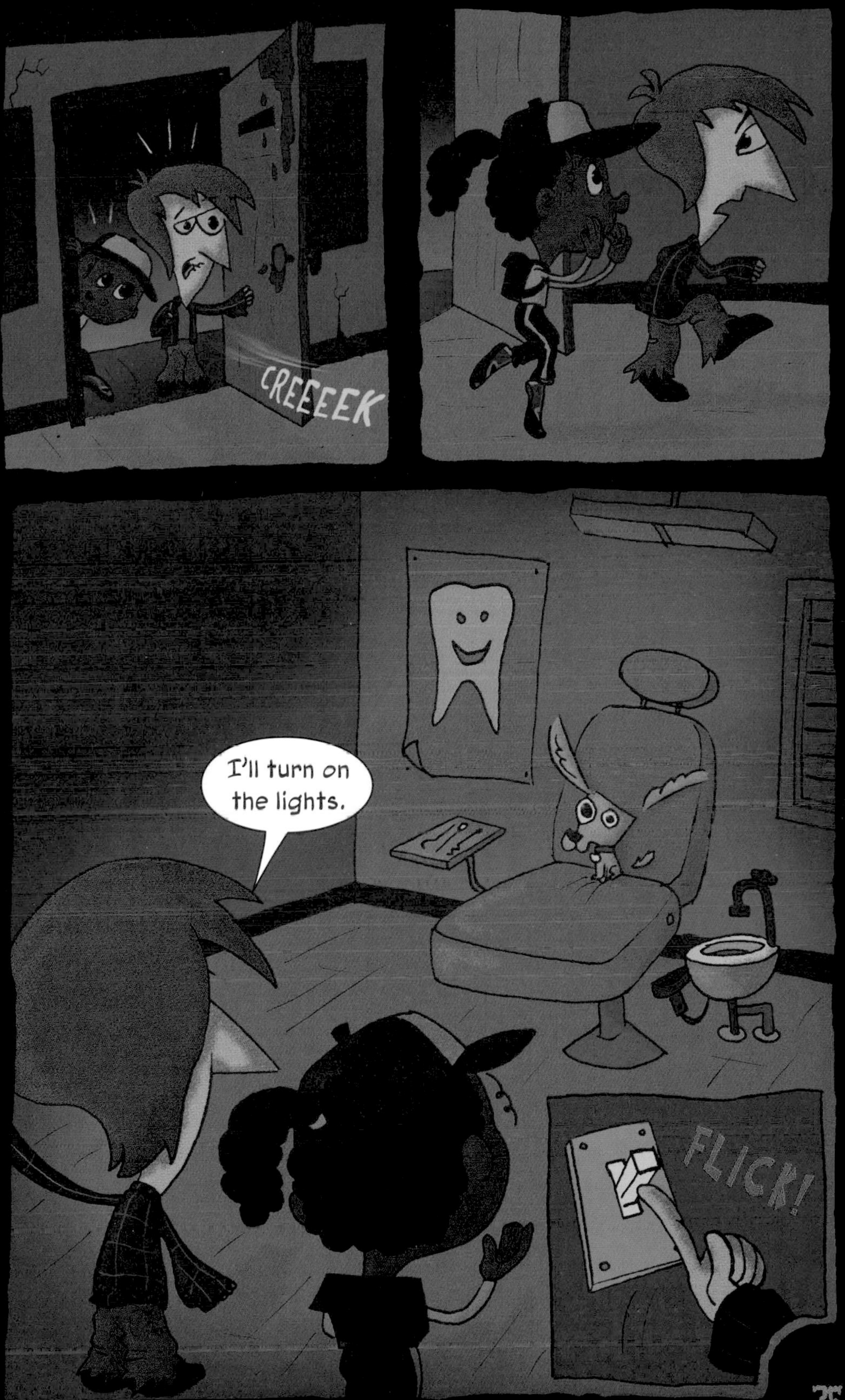
CREEEEEK
I'll turn on the lights.
FLICK!

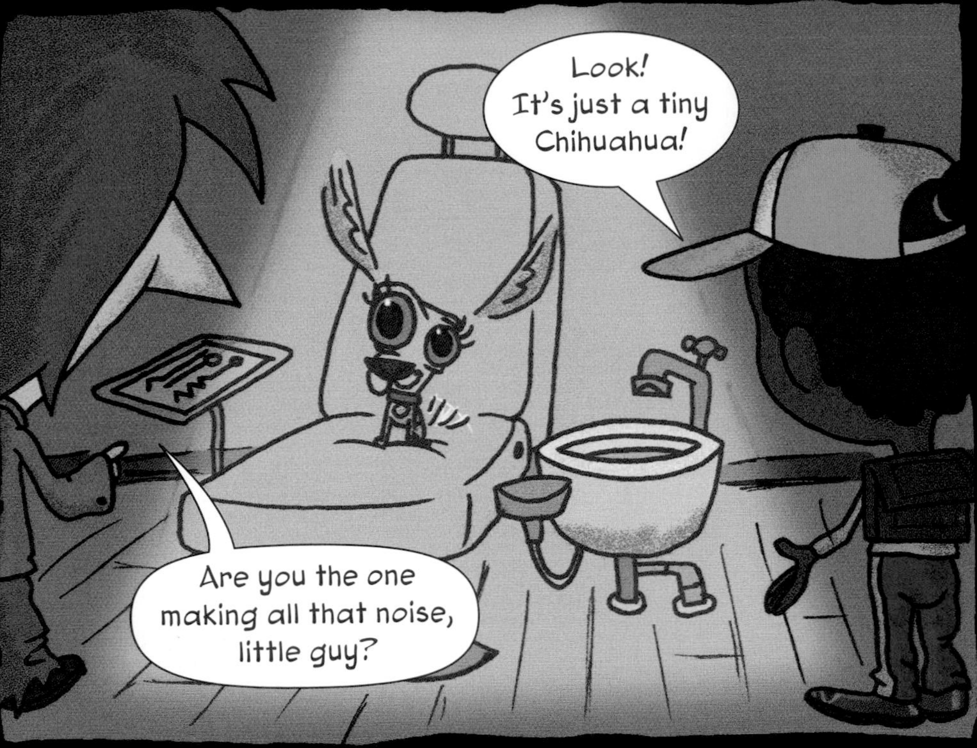
Look!
It's just a tiny
Chihuahua!
Are you the one
making all that noise,
little guy?

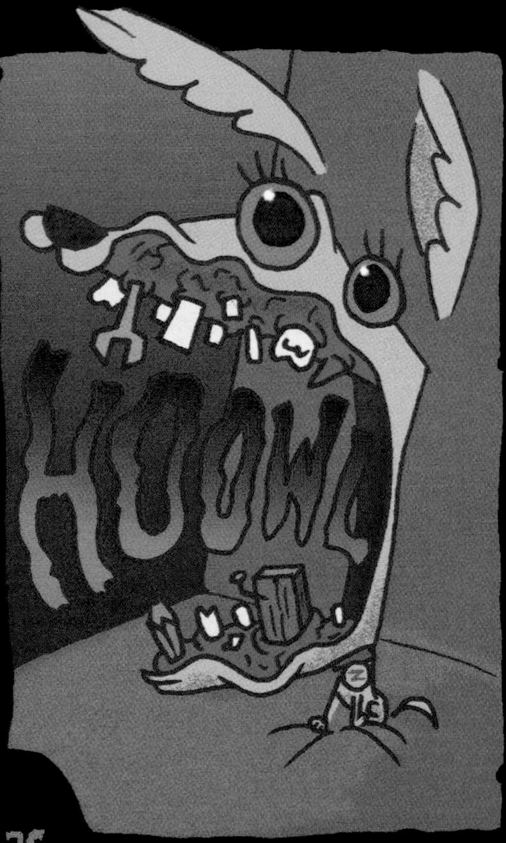
HOOOWL

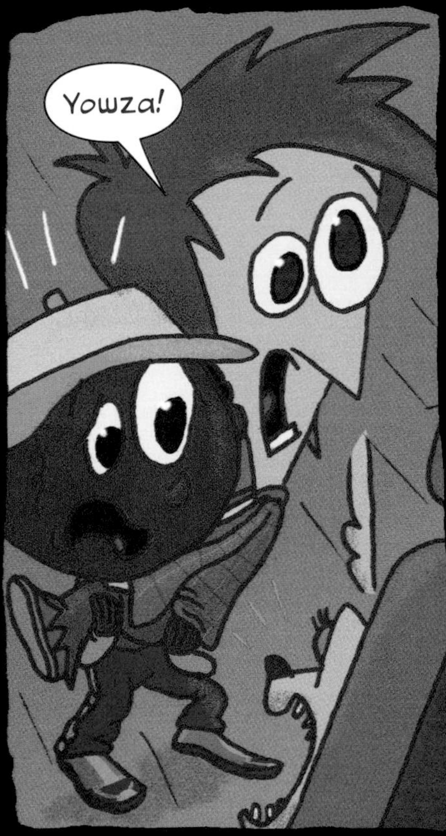
Yowza!

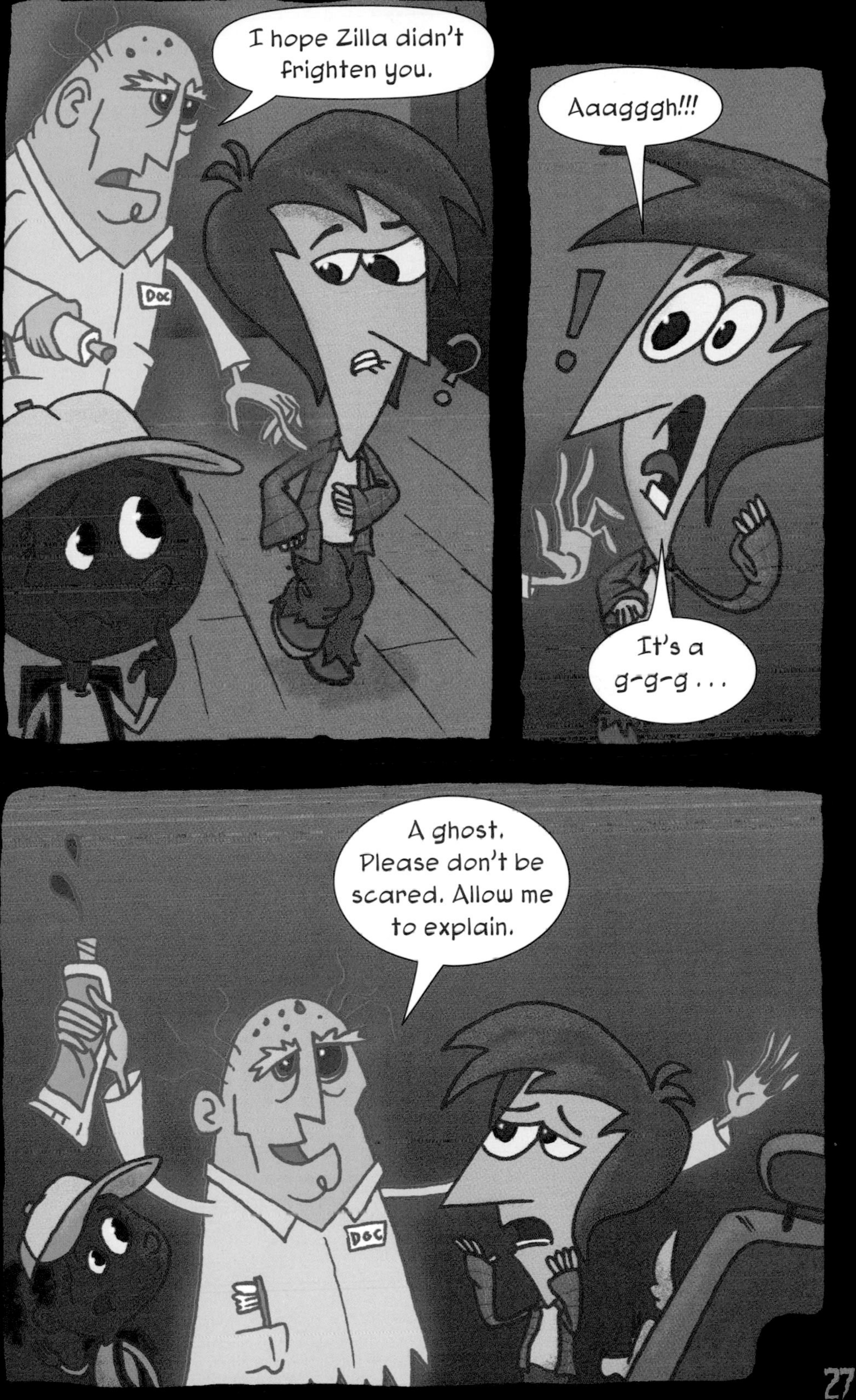

I hope Zilla didn't frighten you.
Aaagggh!!!
It's a g-g-g . . .
A ghost. Please don't be scared. Allow me to explain.

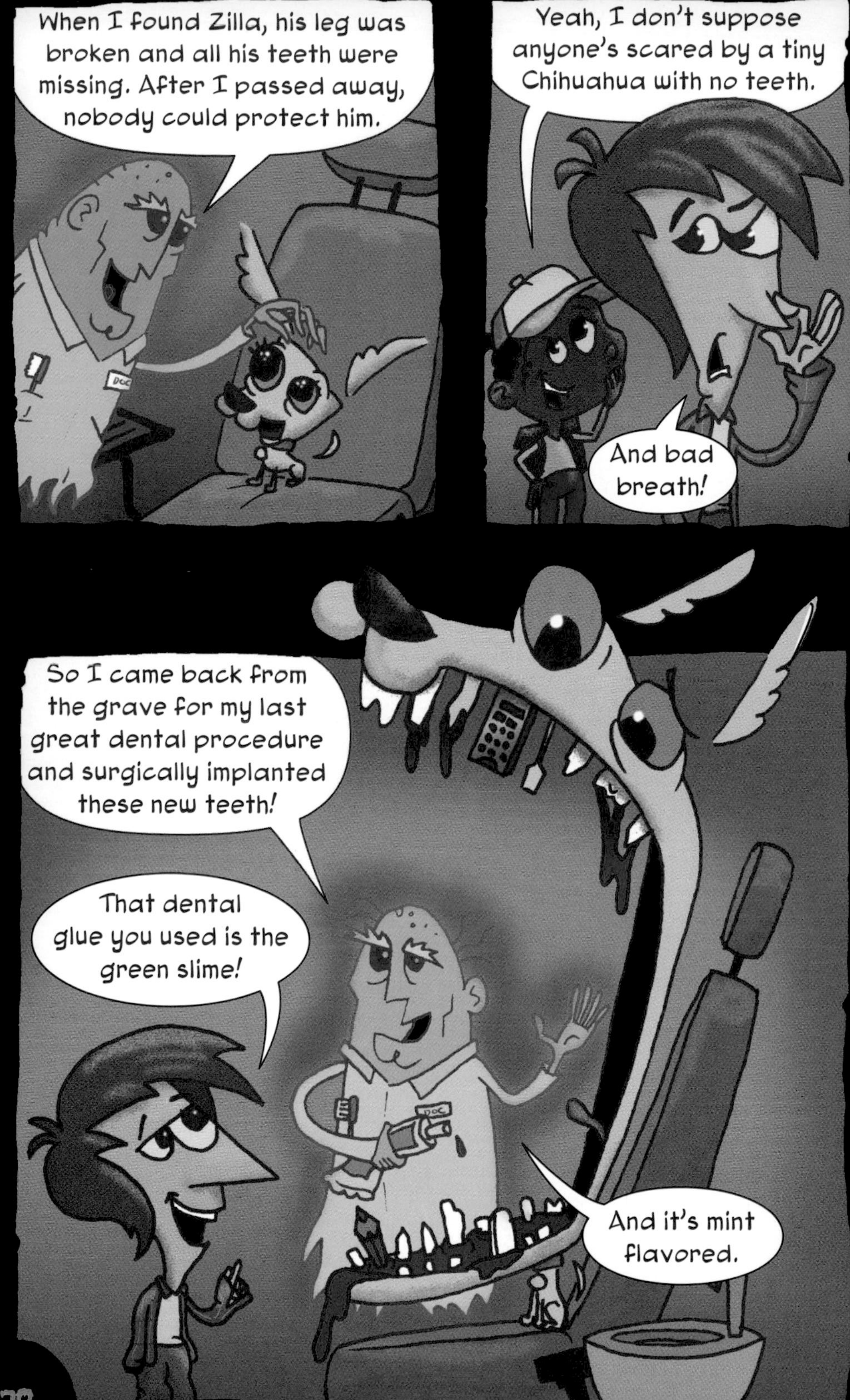
When I found Zilla, his leg was broken and all his teeth were missing. After I passed away, nobody could protect him.
Yeah, I don't suppose anyone's scared by a tiny Chihuahua with no teeth.
And bad breath!
So I came back from the grave for my last great dental procedure and surgically implanted these new teeth!
That dental glue you used is the green slime!
And it's mint flavored.

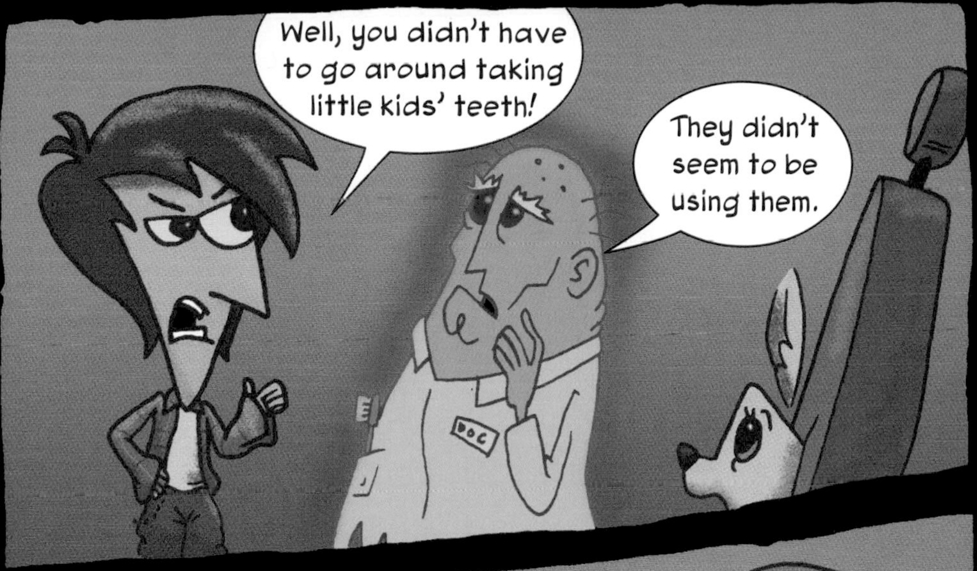
Well, you didn't have to go around taking little kids' teeth!
They didn't seem to be using them.
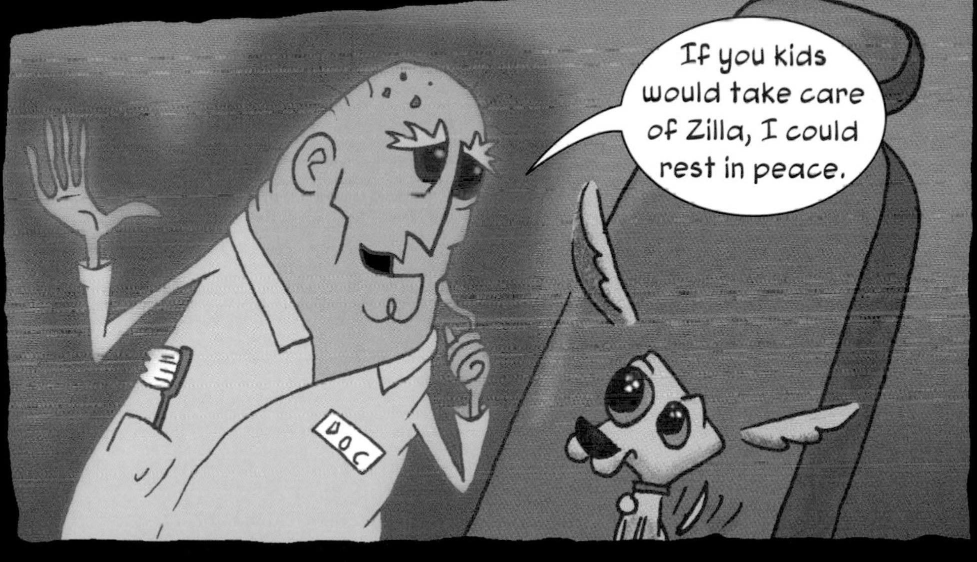
If you kids would take care of Zilla, I could rest in peace.
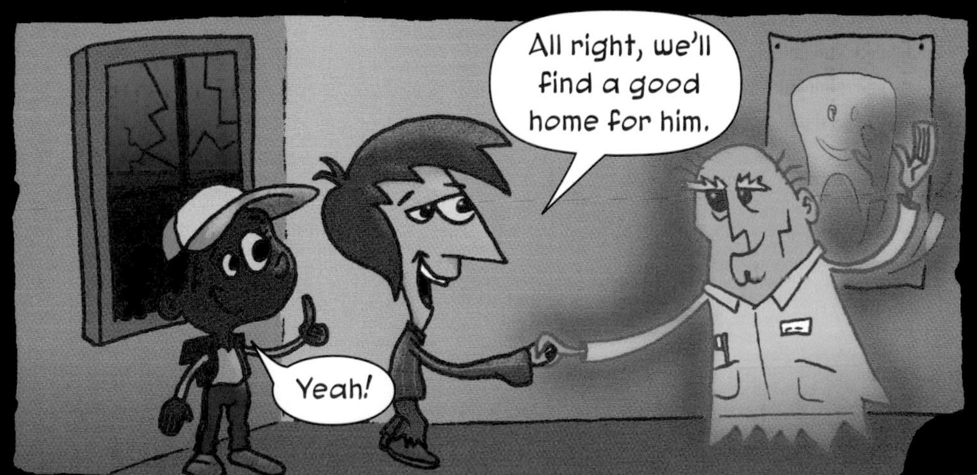
All right, we'll find a good home for him.
Yeah!

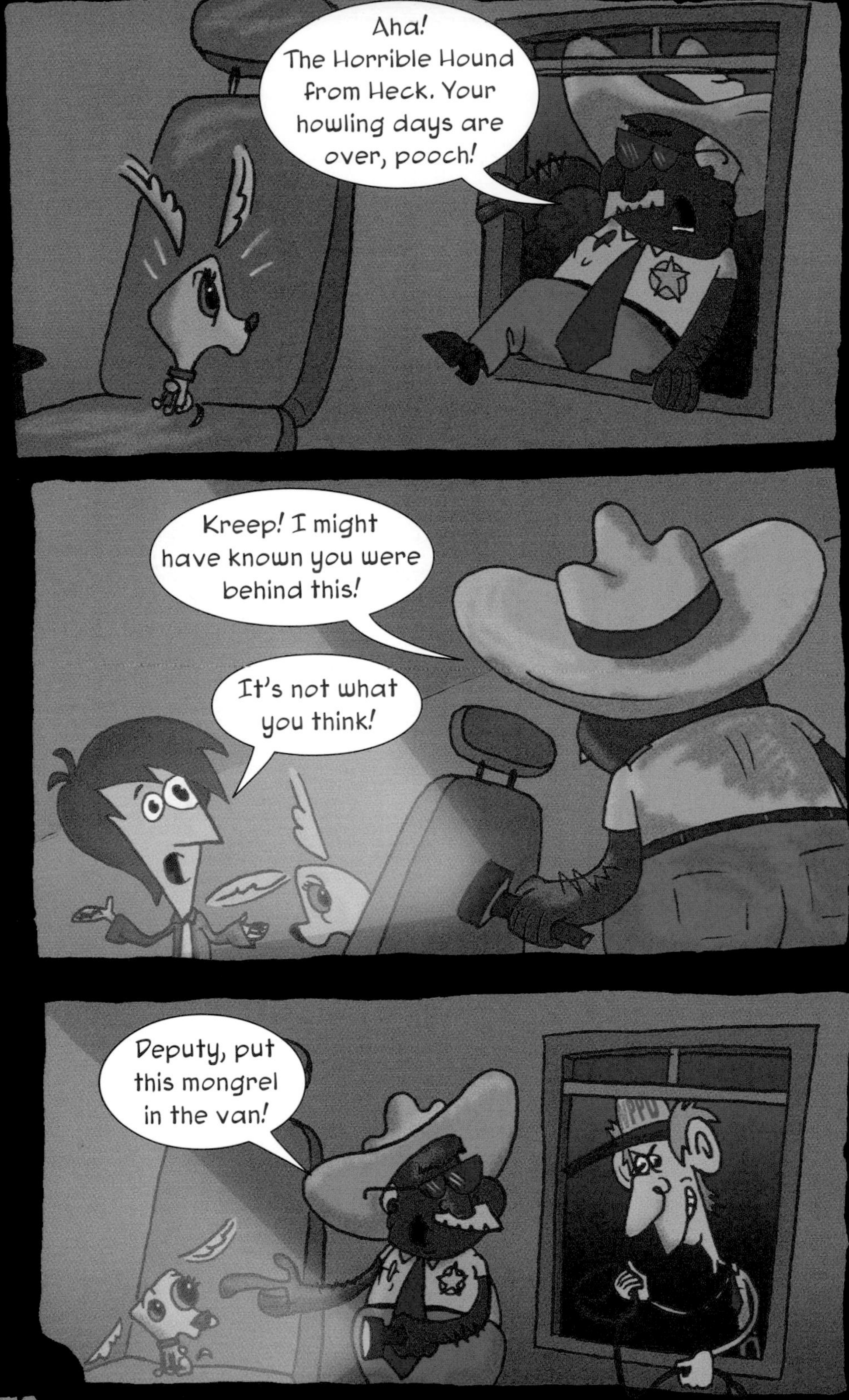
Aha! The Horrible Hound from Heck. Your howling days are over, pooch!
Kreep! I might have known you were behind this!
It's not what you think!
Deputy, put this mongrel in the van!
PPD

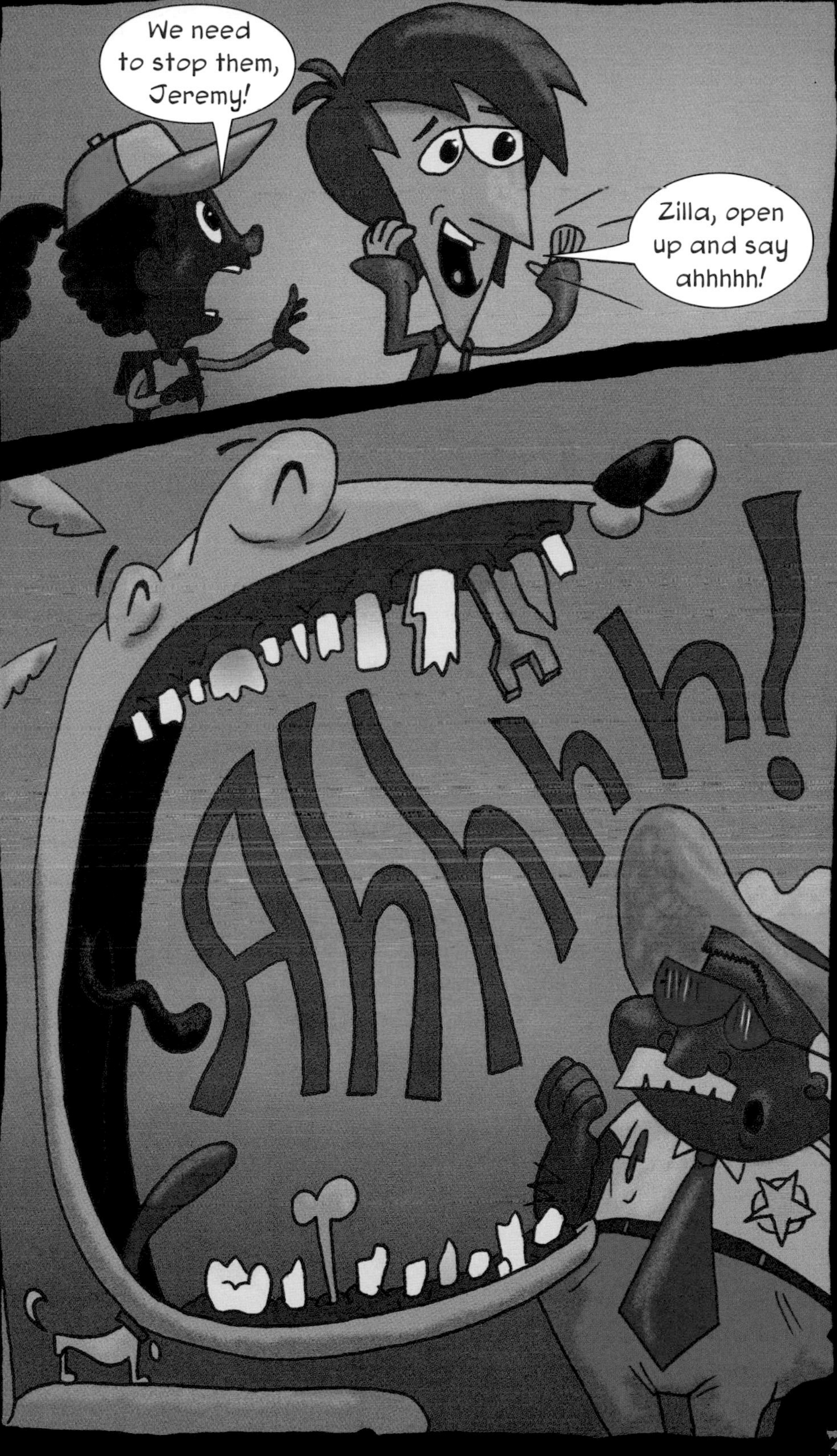
We need to stop them, Jeremy!
Zilla, open up and say ahhhhh!
Ahhhh!

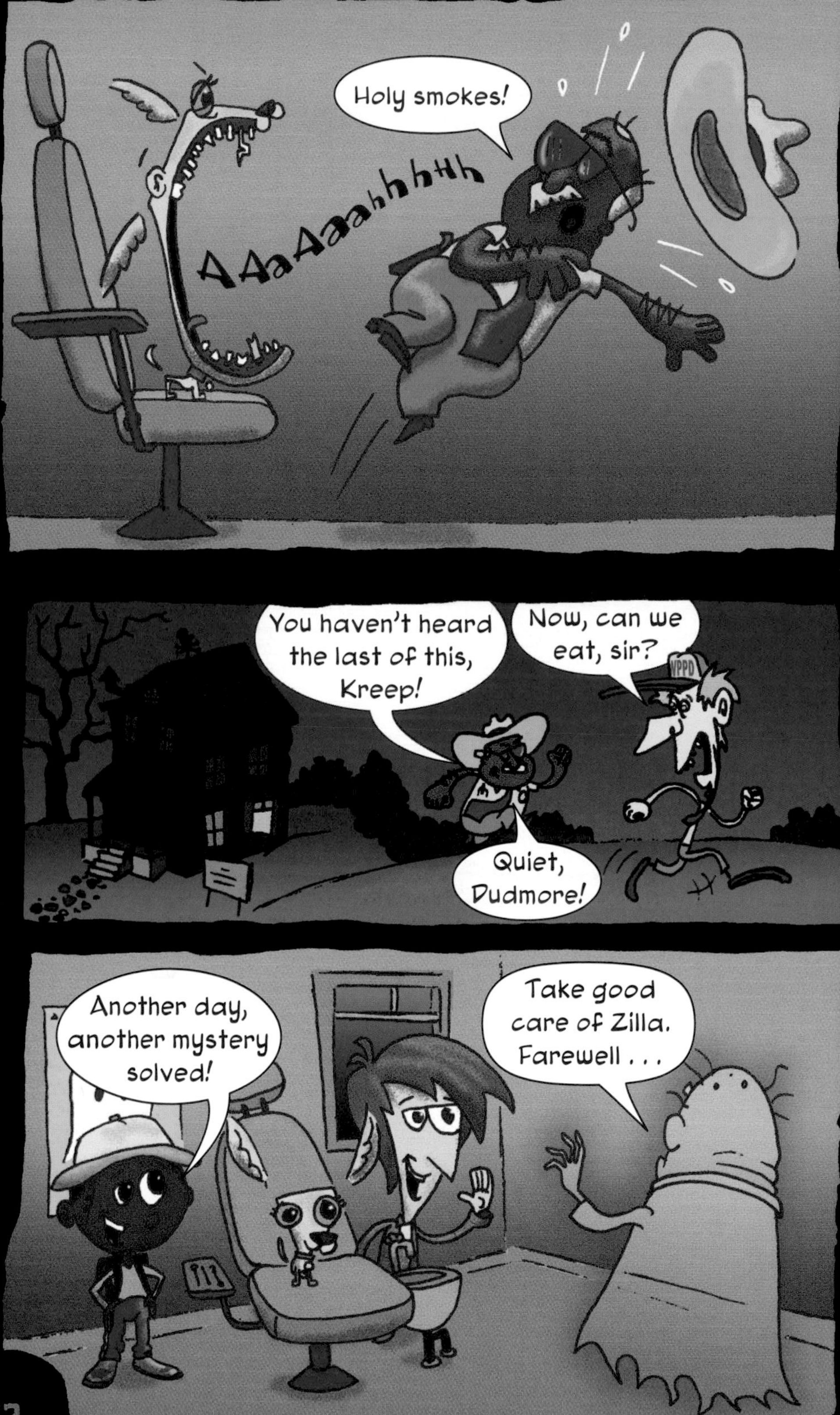
Holy smokes!
AAaAaaahhhhh
You haven't heard the last of this, Kreep!
Now, can we eat, sir?
VPPD
Quiet, Dudmore!
Another day, another mystery solved!
Take good care of Zilla. Farewell . . .

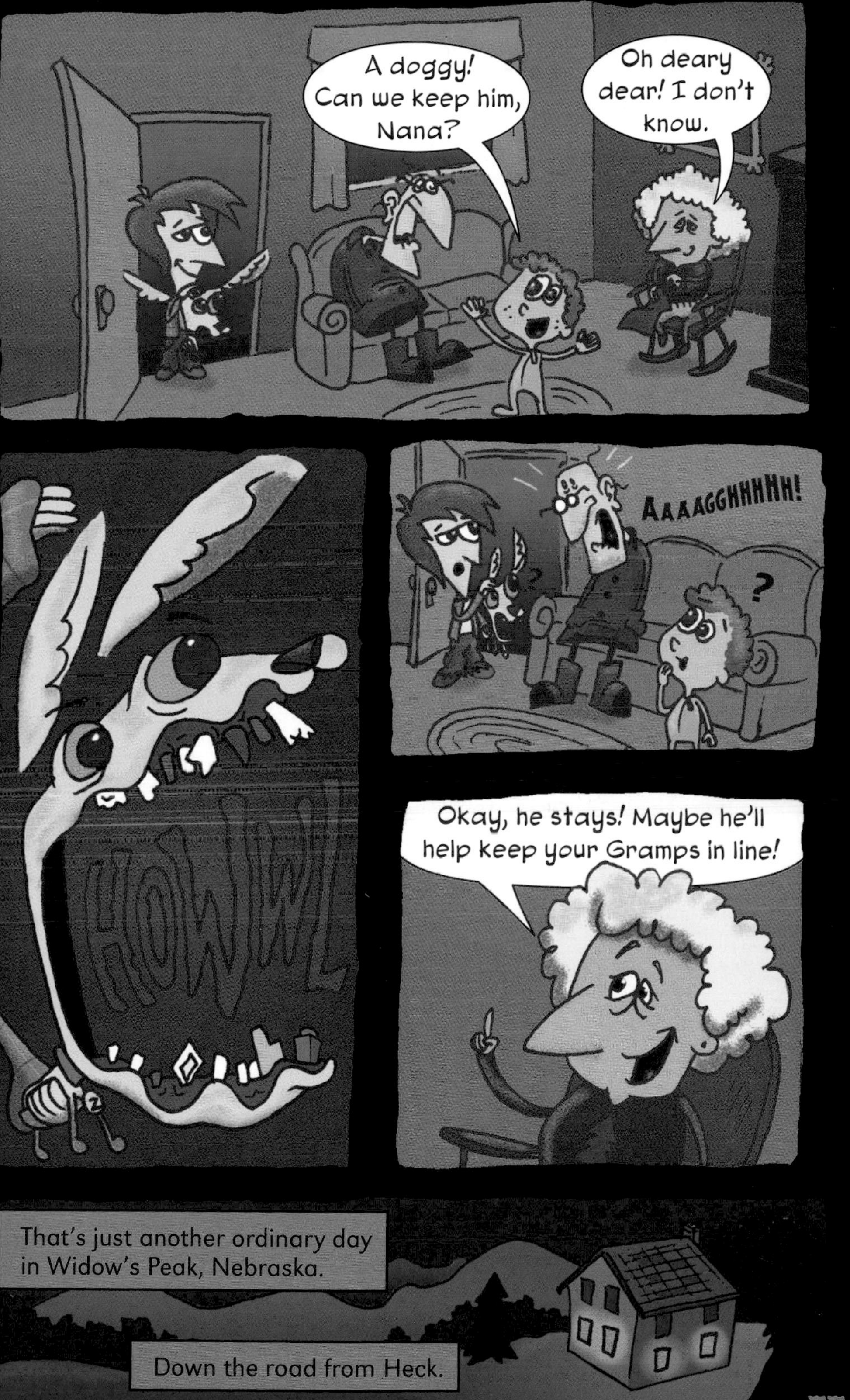
A doggy! Can we keep him, Nana?
Oh deary dear! I don't know.
HOWWL
AAAAGGHHHHH!
?
Okay, he stays! Maybe he'll help keep your Gramps in line!
That's just another ordinary day in Widow's Peak, Nebraska.
Down the road from Heck.

ABOUT THE AUTHOR AND ILLUSTRATOR

From a young age, Andy Smith knew he wanted to be an illustrator (if he couldn't be a space adventurer, superhero, or ghost hunter). After graduating from college in 1998, he began working at a handful of New York City animation studios on shows like *Courage the Cowardly Dog* and *Sheep in the Big City*, while also working in freelance illustration. Andy has since left New York City for Rochester, NY, where he teaches high school art and illustration at the Rochester Institute of Technology.

Where's the dollar for my tooth, Mr. Smith?

GLOSSARY

Chihuahua (chi-WAH-wah)—a breed of very small dogs with big eyes and pointed ears

digital camera (DIJ-uh-tul KAM-ur-uh)—a machine that captures photographs electronically instead of using film. A digital camera stores its pictures on a computer chip.

evidence (EV-uh-duhnss)—facts or info that help prove that something is true

mongrel (MONG-gruhl)—a dog that is a mixture of different breeds

stakeout (STAYK-out)—watching an area to catch a criminal in the act

tofu (TOH-foo)—a soft food made from soybeans

willies (WIHL-eez)—a nervous feeling about a situation; also called the **jitters**, the **heebie-jeebies,** and the **creepy crawlies**.

yowza (YOW-zuh)—something you might say when you get the willies!

SOME TOOTH TRUTH

Here are just a few truths about the tooth.

Like Zilla the Chihuahua, the first U.S. president, George Washington, had fake teeth. Many believe they were made from wood. They were actually made from gold, ivory, lead, and even whale bone!

Don't blame Washington for his bad teeth, though. The first modern toothbrush wasn't invented until 1780 in England. Americans didn't start brushing daily for another 150 years!

Before the first toothbrush, people kept their teeth clean by chewing on twigs.

In parts of the world, straight, white teeth are not popular. People in some Asian countries color their teeth black. In some parts of Africa, people file their teeth into sharp points.

Humans get two sets of teeth in their lifetime. The first set of 20 teeth are often called primary teeth, baby teeth, or milk teeth.

Grown-up humans have 32 teeth, but dogs have that number beat. Adult dogs have 42 teeth.

Around the world, children have different ways for getting rid of teeth that fall out. In the United States, kids often leave them under a pillow for the tooth fairy. Other countries have a "tooth mouse" that scurries around collecting baby teeth. Some South American children even have their old teeth made into jewelry.

DISCUSSION QUESTIONS

1.) Jeremy and Nessy were scared when they first met Zilla the Chihuahua. Have you ever judged someone on how they look? Do you think this is wrong? Why?

2.) Dr. Crenshaw's ghost stole children's teeth to help Zilla the Chihuahua. Is stealing ever okay? Explain your answer.

3.) Why do you think the author chose a Chihuahua as the Hound from Heck? Explain your answer. What type of dog would you have chosen?

WRITING PROMPTS

1.) Zilla howls like a wolf and has some pretty wacky teeth. List three things that make your own pet or your friend's pet unique. Write a story about the pet using these three features.

2.) Have you ever tried to solve a mystery like Jeremy and Nessy did? Did you solve it? Describe the mystery and your solution.

3.) This story focuses on just one day in the town of Widow's Peak, Nebraska. Write a story about another day in the strange town. What crazy things happen on that day?

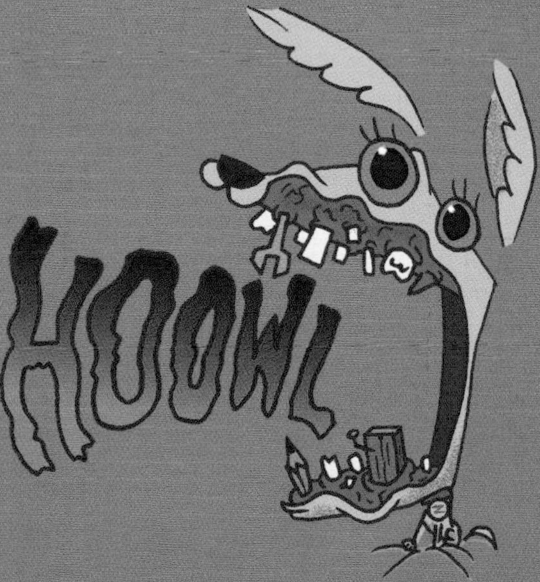
HOOWL

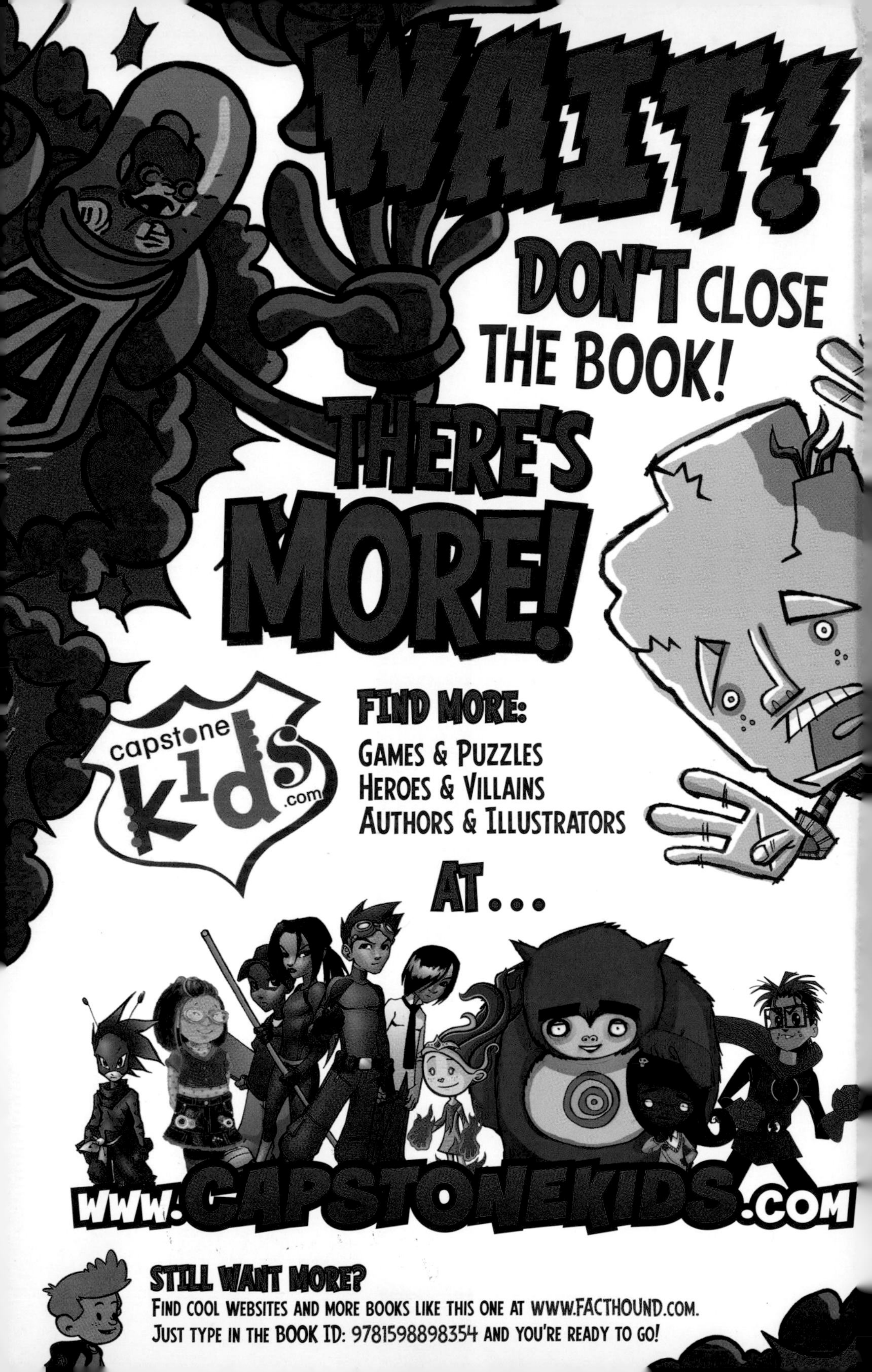
WAIT!
DON'T CLOSE THE BOOK!
THERE'S MORE!
capstone kids .com
FIND MORE:
GAMES & PUZZLES
HEROES & VILLAINS
AUTHORS & ILLUSTRATORS
AT...
WWW.CAPSTONEKIDS.COM
STILL WANT MORE?
FIND COOL WEBSITES AND MORE BOOKS LIKE THIS ONE AT WWW.FACTHOUND.COM.
JUST TYPE IN THE BOOK ID: 9781598898354 AND YOU'RE READY TO GO!